**And the Baker's Boy
Went to Sea**

And the Baker's Boy Went to Sea

Mary Cummings

SPARKLING PRESS
St. Paul, Minnesota

Sparkling Press
137 East Curtice Street
St. Paul, MN 55107
sparklingpress@peoplepc.com

Design by Dorie McClelland, Spring Book Design
Illustration Credits:
Cutaway showing compartmentation of a typical U.S. submarine, from Eugene B. Fluckey, *Thunder Below! The USS Barb Revolutionizes Submarine Warfare in World War II;* Copyright 1992 by the Board of Trustees of the University of Illinois. Used with permission of the University of Illinois Press, and the author.
Photo of dolphins pin, Courtesy Paul Cummings and Dorie McClelland.
All other photos, Courtesy National Archives.

Publisher's Cataloging-in-Publication
(Provided by Quality Books, Inc.)
Cummings, Mary.
  And the baker's boy went to sea / Mary Cummings. —
1st ed.
  p. cm.
  Includes bibliographical references.
  SUMMARY: Fifteen-year-old Owen, too young to enlist in the U.S. Navy, lies about his age and joins the crew of a WWII submarine. But just like at home, he is assigned to bake bread. He envies his older friends who serve as lookout and gunner, as the crew hunts Japanese ships.
  Audience: Ages 10-14.
  LCCN 2005938813
  ISBN-10: 0-9774855-0-1
  ISBN-13: 978-0-9774855-0-5
  1. United States. Navy—Submarine forces—Juvenile fiction. 2. World War, 1939–1945—Naval operations—Submarine—Juvenile fiction. [1. United States. Navy—Submarine forces—Fiction. 2. World War, 1939–1945—Fiction. 3. Submarine warfare—Fiction. 4. Submarines (Ships)—Fiction.] I. Title.
  PZ7.C9135And 2006   [E]
                QBI06-600017

Printed in the United States of America
Printed on acid-free paper
First edition 2006

For my father, Paul Cummings,
Who served four war patrols on the
U.S.S. *Blackfish*
And for my mother, Lorayne Cummings,
Who awaited his return

—M. C.

This book was inspired and aided by the accounts of many submarine veterans of World War II. The author especially extends thanks to:

Paul Cummings, U.S.S. *Blackfish*
Dan Decker, U.S.S. *Spadefish*
Robert Gillette, U.S.S. *Lapon* and U.S.S. *Blackfish*
Billy Grieves, U.S.S. *Thresher*
Robert Hall, U.S.S. *Parche*
Leonard Hill, U.S.S. *Barb*
Grover McLeod, U.S.S. *Finback* and U.S.S. *Halibut*
The late Norman Ostrom, U.S.S. *Skate*
Fred Richards, U.S.S. *Parche*
The late Cliff Robinson, U.S.S. *Plunger*
James Ross, U.S.S. *Blackfish*
Pete Sencenbaugh, U.S.S. *Raton*
Roland Soucy, U.S.S. *Rasher*
Frank Vice, U.S.S. *Blackfish*
Carl Vozniak U.S.S. *Parche* and U.S.S. *Finback*
Donald Walters, U.S.S. *Parche*

Thanks also to Jerry Calenberg, Submarine Technician; to staff and volunteers of the Wisconsin Maritime Museum; to my husband and daughter, Tom and Ada Breitenbucher; to the authors of the many books on World War II submarines consulted in the writing of this novel; and to my friends and writing mentors at The Loft Literary Center.

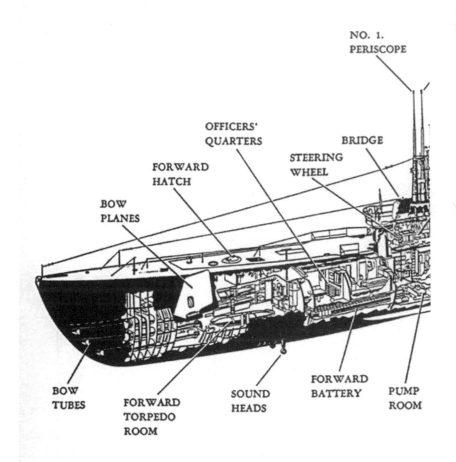

NO. 1.
PERISCOPE

OFFICERS'
QUARTERS

BRIDGE

STEERING
WHEEL

FORWARD
HATCH

BOW
PLANES

BOW
TUBES

FORWARD
TORPEDO
ROOM

SOUND
HEADS

FORWARD
BATTERY

PUMP
ROOM

Cutaway showing compartmentation of a typical U.S. submarine

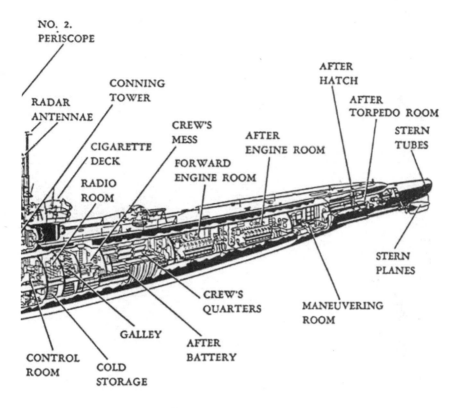

NO. 2.
PERISCOPE

AFTER
HATCH

RADAR
ANTENNAE

CONNING
TOWER

AFTER
TORPEDO ROOM

CREW'S
MESS

AFTER
ENGINE ROOM

STERN
TUBES

CIGARETTE
DECK

FORWARD
ENGINE ROOM

RADIO
ROOM

STERN
PLANES

CREW'S
QUARTERS

MANEUVERING
ROOM

GALLEY

CONTROL
ROOM

COLD
STORAGE

AFTER
BATTERY

Owen Pasquerly crouched between the garbage cans outside the bakery's back door. He scooped up some dirty snow and cupped it below his ear. Little bursts of pain swirled and collided with the dense, numbing cold seeping into his neck. He stared at a small patch of driveway in front of him. Thin snow drifted down, dusting the pebbles and potholes until they almost couldn't be seen anymore.

The buzz of the radio inside with the latest warfront news mixed with the *whirr thwap whirr whirr* of the rusty fan above the ovens. It was a sound he knew so well he didn't even really hear it. But Owen's nose caught the smell of burnt bread blown out the fan into the January morning. Pop started cursing. Heaved a pan at the wall. Owen felt its thud against his curved back. He tensed, ready to bolt, the welt on his neck pulsing madly.

The last thing Owen wanted was for people to stare and ask, "What in the Sam Hill happened to you?" Owen wondered how their faces would look if he said, "This time I didn't duck when Pop came at me. Pop—you know—that nice man who jokes with his bakery customers. Who hates his own son."

Owen squeezed his eyes shut. Like a movie with the film stuck and jerking, he was in the bakery again and it was half an hour ago. Owen saying something offhand about Pop's rolls looking lopsided. Pop rearing up like a grizzly bear, his eyes red. "You goddamn runt kid—don't you never sass your old man!" Pop's enormous fist coming at him, expecting Owen to duck like he always did. But Owen knew our men out in the war wouldn't duck. So this time, he just looked into Pop's eyes, willing the fist to fall limp. Pop's amazed shame, then volcanic anger. The fist rolling over the edge of Owen's jaw, like a boulder crashing into his neck. Pop staring, panting. Owen out the back door.

Owen startled as he heard a pull on the cowbell from the front of the bakery. A customer had walked in. Pop was losing his hearing a little at a time, but the bell clanked loud enough. Owen pictured a worm inside Pop's ear, eating the hearing parts.

Pop for sure wouldn't come after Owen now. He sank back into the shelter of the garbage cans, shivering arms wrapped around his legs. He looked down at his toes. Small feet. *Runt kid. Pop's right. Won't ever be as big as Pop. And my face. Like an explosion in the freckles factory. Like Ma's face.*

A pair of scuffed brown shoes stopped in front of him. Owen looked up.

"Got you this time, didn't he?"

Owen nodded. It was Gary Crowley, Owen's best friend. Gary squatted down beside him.

"I remember when he was a good guy, a regular dad to you," said Gary.

"Me too—but it's getting harder to remember." Owen let the snow pack drop from his neck into his lap.

"Let's talk about getting away from here. About joining up for the war, if we could," said Owen. "What would you want to do?"

"Aw, you ask me that every week."

"Yeah. But tell me anyway."

"A flier. Go on missions over Europe. Or maybe Japan. I already know what you'd want to do," said Gary.

"I'd go to sea. On a submarine. Just like in *Destination Tokyo*. Those guys were a team—they weren't scared of nothin'."

"Owen . . . ," said Gary. "I was seventeen last month, you know. When a guy's seventeen he can join up if his folks give permission."

Owen jerked his head. "They said yes? You're going?"

"Yup. I'm all set."

No more Gary. Owen felt a stone plunge to the bottom of his stomach.

"Hey, don't look so gloomy," said Gary, jumping to his feet. "I figured out how to get you into the Navy!"

"I'm fifteen. Have you forgotten that? War'll be over with by the time I'm old enough to see some action. They're not going to take a fifteen-year-old."

"I know. I know. That's what took some figuring. Now, you were born over in Helena, right?"

"You know I was," replied Owen. "So what?'

"So—you pick a town up on the Highline."

"I pick a town?"

"Yeah. And you write them a letter. Do it on a typewriter. You say you were born in that town in 1927. It's 1944 now, so that would make you seventeen. Tell them a date—in January." Gary's eyes gleamed.

"I say I was born there? In 1927?"

3

"Yeah! Don't you see? You tell them you need a certificate of your birth date. Of course, they won't be able to find one, but they won't think that's so strange because lots of births are done at home up there. Their records aren't so good because of that."

"And they'd believe me?" asked Owen.

"Other guys have done it and it's worked."

"So what then?"

"Then you get a paper in the mail that says you were born there, when you said you were. Or a blank for you to fill in and get a parent to sign. So you'll have something that says you're seventeen. You take it to the recruiting officer, down at the post office, and you're set. That is—if you get the form signed. You can manage that, can't you?" asked Gary.

Owen's brain worked fast. If Pop was drunk, he'd start hollering about how he'd like to get rid of his runty son, and he'd sign anything. Or, if it was Ma—he didn't want to trick Ma. He'd find a way, though. "Yup," he replied, taking quick breaths.

"So I'll be up there somewhere in the sky, and you'll be way down, under the ocean. Maybe I'll fly right over you and won't even know it," laughed Gary.

Owen shuddered like a deer kept in a pen, seeing an open gate.

Soon he'd see the ocean for the first time.

He'd fight our enemies on the high seas.

And he'd get away from Pop.

L O C A T I O N: New London, Connecticut.
Submarine School
Enrique Romero
At the Window Seat

Enrique Romero heaved an exasperated sigh. In the time since leaving his buddy Nick Gallagher, he'd gone outside and drawn a diagram in the dirt of the parts of a torpedo, eaten a candy bar, and flipped through his class notes. Now he was back at the window seat in the old barracks. Nick was exactly—precisely—where Enrique had left him an hour ago.

"How can you sit there for so long just staring at a book?"

Without moving anything except his mouth, Nick replied, "I'm not staring, Romeo. I'm studying."

"You're like a statue, Nicky. You're driving me nuts."

"You got nuts a long time ago. Now go away," replied Nick, still not moving. "We've got that test tomorrow, remember? Lieutenant Baine's not going to let us off easy."

Enrique could never sit still for long. He liked noise and fast, jazzy music and was used to living in a city. Nick was from a farm up north. Enrique had never been on a farm in his life. He wondered if all farm people were like this. He was still figuring Nick out. They hadn't known each other all that long. And studying for hours was no fun.

"Let you study? Sure I'll let you study!" yelled Enrique, yanking *The Fleet Submarine: Design and Operation Specifications* from Nick. Nick grabbed at it, his fingertips jabbing the air as the book spun overhead, before landing with a thud.

Nick's face darkened. "Cut it out, Romeo! Maybe you know all this stuff, but I don't. Maybe you're just smarter than some people!" He kicked toward Enrique, at the same time sliding into the corner of the window seat. He was breathing hard.

"I'm not smarter than—other people," said Enrique, looking wide-eyed at Nick. He almost said, "I'm not smarter than you," except he knew that in some ways he was smarter because he could read something a couple of times and remember it. Nick couldn't. Or, maybe Nick figured he couldn't and got tensed up. But when it came to learning practical things, from machines— that was different. Enrique had seen him in the simulator room at sub school, where they got to practice on actual engines and diving controls. Nick was tops at that.

"Nicky, how come you want this so bad?" said Enrique, before he even knew he was going to ask the question.

"Want what?" muttered Nick.

"To be on a submarine. You never told me about that."

"Well, you never told me, either."

"I guess we both have our reasons. There's easier ways to be in the war than to go through sub school," said Enrique.

"Yeah, there are," agreed Nick. "But I got it figured. We get top pay being on a submarine—especially once we qualify for our dolphins."

"You thinking about qualifying, too? Those dolphins will look sharp—I can hardly wait to sew them on and show the girls—"

Nick snorted. "For me, it ain't about showing the girls. We need the money for the farm. To get more cows and machinery." Nick began to speak faster, excitedly. "Not just tractors, you know. Farming's changing."

Enrique had never thought about farms. "You're doing all this studying for machines? And cows?"

Nick stared back. "Sure I am. A farmer's what I'm going to be. I'll learn about fixing motors and compressors on a submarine to help on the farm. Aren't you doing this for your family, too? I mean, partly anyhow?"

Enrique was silent. His reasons were all mixed up. He shrugged.

"I wanted to be in on the action. Not enough happening at home. To be away in the war, and people would read about where I was in the newspaper and battles I was winning."

"Me too," said Nick. "And to see the ocean. There's lots of lakes in Minnesota, but I never been to the ocean before."

Enrique was only half listening, because he hadn't told everything. He was doing this for his family—only not in the way Nick was. Enrique had to tell somebody about what burned his insides.

"Torpedoes," he said.

"Torpedoes?" asked Nick.

"Yeah. *Whoosh, bubble-bubble* BLAM!" Enrique imitated the sounds of a torpedo shooting out from its tube, moving his arm to show it shimmy in the water, then smacked his hands together.

"I like torpedoes, too—" said Nick.

"And they kill off the Japs," said Enrique. He liked the word "Japs." The cruel, sharp sound it made, like a swear word.

GETTING YOUR DOLPHINS

A shining metal pin, or an arm patch, showing
a submarine flanked by twin dolphins, was
a badge of honor that submariners could
wear only if they earned it. To be "qualified
in submarines" meant a sailor knew how
everything worked on the boat, from engines
to torpedoes, ventilation to electrical systems,
steering to diving—and could help anywhere
in case of emergency. A sailor would keep a
log, drawing in it each of the main systems of
the boat, then be tested by the head of each
compartment and by an officer. If he passed, he
got his dolphins! If he wore it without earning
it, he'd risk being beat up by other sailors.

"I guess they do."

"Yeah, they do. Get even for Juan," said Enrique, his face scrunching up like a fist. "They got Juan."

"Juan?"

"My cousin. In the Army. He got sent to the Philippines. We found out he was sick, but he'd have lived, except for Bataan. My brother Julio—he made it. But not Juan. They were prisoners. Damn Japs made them march through the jungle. Nobody could give water or help anybody else or they'd get shot. So Juan died."

"That's lousy."

"Yeah, lousy." Enrique didn't want to talk anymore about Juan. Thinking about him gave a feeling in his middle like being slugged hard until he bled.

He was going to hunt down those Japs and make them pay.

BUT WHAT ABOUT
JAPANESE AMERICANS?

Many people lumped Japanese and Japanese Americans together during the war. They mistrusted them, and even placed them in internment camps. In fact, Japanese Americans were first and foremost Americans, eager to prove their loyalty to the United States. They were no more in sympathy with General Tojo of Japan than German Americans were with Hitler or Italian Americans with Mussolini.

L O C A T I O N: Shipyards of Manitowoc, Wisconsin
Raff Abbott
Changes

Raff Abbott still wasn't used to the feel of solid ground beneath his feet—even though he'd been back stateside a week. He missed the smells of sailors' sweat and the fumes of diesel oil from the *Oarfish*, the submarine he'd commanded out in the Pacific. He'd been called home to oversee the building of a new submarine. And he would be its captain.

The keel had been laid and some of the framework assembled. It was just big chunks of metal now, but soon she'd be home at sea for eighty men. Valves, pipes, tubes, pegs, and bolts put together just so. It was elegant and complicated: Raff liked that.

She would be called the *Mako*. All U.S. submarines got named for a fish or ocean mammal. The mako is a shark. Swift. Unpredictable. Sometimes aggressive. *Perfect for a war submarine*, thought Raff.

But what about the crew? Maybe this new boat—with a crew that hadn't served with him before, hadn't been battle-

SUBMARINE FACTORIES

Despite its distance from an ocean coastline, Manitowoc, Wisconsin, was chosen as one of several shipbuilding center in the United States in the 1940s to build submarines. Craftsmen worked around the clock to rapidly produce these complicated vessels. While the "skeleton" and keel were laid out for one, in adjacent docks two others would be in production.

tested together—would work out fine. Maybe, thought Raff. *But it's a big, dangerous maybe.*

Raff trusted the sailors on the *Oarfish*. It wasn't likely any of them could transfer, but he'd heard he might get Smitty, who, besides being cook on the *Oarfish*, was Raff's friend. But how about a baker? Good bakers were hard to come by. And officers? Torpedomen? Whoever they'd be, he'd meet them soon.

Raff's new lieutenant came first. "Good to meet you, Skipper," said Charlie Zelks. He held out his hand to Raff's. It wasn't one of those bone-crushing handshakes where the other guy is trying to prove something, and it wasn't wilty like somebody acting humble. Raff was going to like this guy. Good thing, too, because he'd have to rely a lot on him.

"Cap'n," announced Charlie the next morning, "the new junior officer is here. He's stashing his gear and he'll be here in an hour."

"Did we get lucky?"

"Well, luck I don't know about. What I know is he's straight out of sub school. Hasn't been to sea."

Raff rolled his eyes—those alien-looking green eyes that intimidated so many people, but not Charlie.

There were too many unknowns with new people. Raff wanted his old *Oarfish* guys back.

Raff drummed his fingers on his desk. He was on the phone arguing with the Bureau of Ordnance about what torpedoes the *Mako* would carry. He wanted twelve Mark XIVs and twelve of the new Mark XVIIIs. What was complicated about that? He wanted to shout and swear. He didn't. But it wasn't the perfect

Constructing submarines

moment for the least experienced, most junior officer assigned to the *Mako* to step through the door.

"Ensign Paul Anderson reporting for duty, sir."

Raff frowned, then turned away. Paul's arm was a straight line from his shoulder, his hand shaping to a smart, crisp salute.

Raff was ready to stay on the phone all day—all week—until he got what he needed. When he finally hung up the telephone, Paul's arm was trembling, but he held the salute.

"Well, Ensign. You've got good form. I'll say that. At ease. I'm Rafferty Abbott. It's Paul, did you say?"

Paul nodded, as he dropped his arm and relaxed.

"Have a seat. Tell me about yourself. How did you come to sign on for subs?" It wasn't chitchat. Raff could learn a lot about a fellow's personality by how he answered.

Paul propped his elbows onto his knees, and began to rub his hands together.

"I decided right from when the war started I liked the idea of the Navy. Every night after dinner my family would listen to the radio, to hear what was going on in the Pacific. It was the Battle of Midway that made me go for submarines."

"And why was that?"

Paul gazed out the window. "A submarine isn't big. But with everyone working together, they make a difference. At Midway, it looked like the Japanese would whip us good. But we had our carriers, our battleships—and nineteen submarines. They each did their part. And when it was done . . . well, the submarines didn't get much of the glory, but they helped tip the scales. So being on a submarine . . . it's doing something small to change something big." He paused. "Do you know what I mean, sir?"

TORPEDOES

A Mark XIV torpedo is faster than a Mark
XVIII, although it leaves a wake, or trail, of
bubbles that could be spotted by a target, giving
it time to evade. But a Mark XVIII can't be fired
from as far away as the XIV. So, each type has
its advantages and disadvantages.

Raff did know. He'd learned all about that on the *Oarfish*.

"Paul," said Raff, "as junior officer, you'll oversee the cook and baker, including supplies and storage. It's not very glamorous, but it's important. Plus, I'm thinking I'll assign you to be boarding officer."

Paul looked confused.

"I know, I know. That regulation's made for surface ships. A submarine almost never has to board another vessel, but we need someone anyway. Do you see any problems?"

"No, sir."

"Good. Now, I must ask that you leave me. I have a memo to get out about our torpedoes."

After Paul left, Raff swiveled back and forth in his desk chair. He didn't write his memo. He wanted to think awhile. *CRREEEEK crick, CREEEEEK crick*, went the old chair. He veered it toward the window, for a view of the shipyard. He watched as a piece of the *Mako*'s hull was lifted and set in place. The *Mako* was more complete now than she was even a few hours ago.

The *Oarfish* he'd always love. But she wasn't his boat now. Besides, a lot of the sailors he'd known there had new assignments someplace else. Things had changed. The *Mako* was his boat. Charlie, Paul—and the others who'd be coming soon—they were his men. And that was just fine.

L O C A T I O N: Manitowoc, Wisconsin.
Lake Michigan.
Owen Pasquerly
Loading Up

Owen stood—ignored—on the submarine's deck, clutching his orders in a sweaty hand. All around him, sailors were loading the boat with torpedoes and supply crates before heading out to sea. Everybody seemed to know what they were supposed to do and where they were supposed to be. Everybody except Owen.

This wasn't like in *Destination Tokyo* that he had seen at the Roxy Theatre. There weren't any friendly guys waiting to shake his hand and welcome him aboard. Gary was far away, learning how to fly. Nobody knew him here, or cared about him.

The hairs on the back of Owen's neck fanned up; he felt somebody watching him. A voice behind him said, "Hey, Buzz, really robbing the cradle with that one, ain't they?" Owen spun around to see two sailors leaning against the dock, smiling sneering smiles at him. His face went hot and he stumbled as he backed away from them, bumping into someone's chest.

"Ooof! It might be smart to watch where you're going, sailor. There's a lot to trip on around here."

TOPSIDE THE SUBMARINE

The "bridge" sticks up from the top of the submarine, rising up from the deck. The periscope and the "shears" which support it are in the center of the bridge. Hatches are circular holes with lids, cut into the deck and bridge to enter and exit the sub. Supplies and torpedoes must also fit down the hatches. Loading a submarine for a war patrol is complicated and needs careful planning.

Owen turned. What he noticed first was a big eagle and gold leaves on the man's cap. What he knew was that this would be the most powerful man in his life now. Not Pop, but someone else to answer to. Maybe to beat him up.

The captain of the U.S.S. *Mako.*

He didn't look anything like Pop. No beer belly, no scowl— but he wasn't smiling, either. He was as tall as Pop, and he looked—strong. He had the strangest eyes Owen had ever seen. Owen tried not to look right into them, because they were green, with an odd brightness. A wizard's eyes searching his face, going all the way through. Could the captain see that he was—officially—too young to be on a submarine?

"I'm Captain Abbott. I haven't seen you on board. Are you . . . assigned to the *Mako?*" asked the captain slowly.

"Yes, sir. The *Mako.*"

"You've been through submarine school?"

"For a little while. They didn't keep me the whole time. Said I was needed."

"Let's see your orders."

Owen unfolded the damp paper and handed it over. The captain glanced at the orders and looked up at Owen.

"You seventeen? Got permission to join up?"

"Yes, sir," replied Owen quickly. It wasn't exactly a lie; he did have Pop's permission. His signature on a paper from when he was drunk, anyway.

"I suppose you're the baker then? We've been waiting for you."

"I am, sir. But I can shoot guns, too."

"Hmm."

Owen watched complicated changes on the captain's face.

He felt small and skinny—even though he'd used hair cream to make his hair stand up. He was afraid of Pop. Should he be afraid of his captain, too?

"Seventeen, eh? You don't exactly look it."

Owen's brain and mouth didn't seem to be connected as he reached for the words he needed to stay here. To go out to sea. What came out was: "Can't . . . help how I look, sir. With respect, sir."

For a moment he wanted to flinch, like when Pop was about to swing at him for sassing. But he'd come this far. He looked right into the captain's face, just like he had that last time at home. The captain just stared some more, before finally saying:

"I suppose you have your reasons for wanting to be here. Kids goof off. Sailors do their jobs. Here's the deal. You study this boat till it spins around in your dreams." He slapped the paper back into Owen's hand. "I don't want any sailor who can't cut it: it's not safe for anybody. You do your baking every night, and you get as good as any sailor on board knowing every system, every gauge, every valve we have—or we kick you off the boat when we get to Australia."

"Yes, sir, I understand. I will."

"Go see the Officer of the Deck—over there. And," he said, a softer look now in his strange eyes, "welcome aboard."

Owen grabbed the grip-bar over the hatch. He twisted himself around in an easy motion onto the ladder that led below deck. He did it casually, as if he'd done it a thousand times. Owen hoped the other sailors noticed.

When he got to the bottom of the ladder, Owen saw a fellow wearing a soft cloth cap with a small stripe on one side. He'd learned this at sub school, but what did this cap mean? Oh, right. An officer. Way below the captain. But still someone in charge.

"I don't think we've met. I'm Mr. Anderson. And you?" Owen knew officers got called "Mr.," even when they weren't very old. The man gripped a clipboard. Papers stuck out every which way under the metal clip.

"I'm Owen Pasquerly. Reporting for duty." He saw Mr. Anderson open his mouth to ask something. Owen didn't want to be questioned again. So he quickly added, "For baking."

"Oh, then you'll want to talk to Smitty. In the galley." He tipped his head to the left. "I have to—" but he stopped as the burly, mean-looking sailor Owen had seen topside pushed his way through the narrow corridor.

The sailor jabbed Owen in the ribs. Hard enough to hurt, but like it could have been an accident. "Move it, Freckle Face," he growled at Owen.

"Where are you going with those cans, Buzz? I mean— Gretz?" Officers were supposed to call fellows by their last name. "I need to know the weight and where all that food's stored so we can be balanced out."

Mr. Anderson was smaller than Buzz Gretz and looked nervous, even though he could boss all the sailors around. Gretz's face was puffy and his eyes half-opened like a toad's. He slid a carton down from his shoulder onto the table next to Owen. It was marked "8–84 oz.—peaches." Gretz sighed like Mr. Anderson had said something stupid.

"I'll see where they fit. Most likely the engine room. Now if you'll excuse me, I got work to do." Gretz paused a moment before adding, "sir," then lifted the heavy crate like it was filled with air.

"Just remember to report in to me later . . ." said Mr. Anderson, flipping through the papers on his clipboard as he walked away.

From just beyond where he stood in the mess—or what land people would call the dining room—Owen heard a loud voice. It came from the galley.

"Fill up the shower with pattatas. Won't be enough fresh water anyway to use it much. You guys can wait a few weeks to get clean, but you want French fries and hash browns, the pattatas need to go someplace. Fill it to the top and board it up except for a trapdoor."

Owen peered around the corner. So that was Smitty. The fellow he was supposed to see.

Smitty turned his head—big and shaggy like a buffalo's, and just as ornery.

"And who might you be, sailor?"

"'Name's Owen Pasquerly, sir."

"Don't 'sir' me. I'm a regular guy, same as you. Elmer Smith. Cook. Call me Smitty. And you? With that hair I guess they call you 'Red' or how about 'Freckles?'"

Owen hated nicknames, especially those two. "People who like me call me 'Owen.' "

Smitty grunted. "You reporting to help stock the food?"

"No, but I guess I could. I'm here because—well, I'm good on guns, but I'm going to do baking."

Smitty folded his arms like Owen better prove it. "You a real baker?" he asked. "You look like a kid."

"Oh, yeah. My family runs a bakery. Back in Montana, I get up pretty much every morning and bake."

"That so? Well, I'll give you a try. It's 'Owen,' eh? Ain't time to find somebody else anyhow." He blew out a breath, making his belly bounce. "We got sailors on duty round the clock and they always want feeding. I cook all day for 'em. You bake all night. You prepared for that?"

"Sure," said Owen, even though he'd never stayed up all night, or baked more than a few times a week. But he wouldn't let on about that.

"All right, then. Mostly we keep our supplies separate. The eggs in the cooler are for breakfast, not baking. You got yer butter down below, but you'll have to fill in with lard. Yeast up here," said Smitty, slapping at a metal cupboard over the tiny sink, "and flour wherever we can squeeze it in—behind the engines, in the pump room—anyplace." Smitty pointed his stubby thumb toward the corridor. "Yer eggs we'll put in the forward escape hatch. That'll keep 'em cool."

Owen pictured eggs cracking and splatting on the heads of sailors trying to escape if they had an emergency.

"You listening to me, sailor?"

"Ah, eggs in the forward escape hatch, yup. Got it," Owen replied.

"Well, make yerself useful then. See all them crates of crackers on the mess tables? Find spaces for them under the crew's bunks. Any that don't fit, stick in the officers' quarters— only be real polite when you go in. And tell Mr. Anderson where yer putting it all. He's gotta keep track. Oh, and tell him how much cinnamon you want for your rolls and things."

Smitty seemed to be starting to think Owen was OK. Just to make conversation, as he braced his legs and lifted a cracker crate, Owen said, "Sure are a lot of crackers. We won't run out of snacks, I guess."

"Crackers ain't just for snacks, my baker friend. When the seas get rough, crackers are what to eat. That way, when you upchuck, they don't scratch yer throat coming up like other things do."

Owen carried the crates one at a time, squeezing cracker boxes in any cubby or corner he could find. Each time he came back for another load, he watched Smitty directing traffic like a cop, sending sailors to store food for the long voyage. Owen began to feel thirsty and leaned over toward the tiny drinking fountain, or "scuttlebutt."

"Hey, there!" yelled Smitty. Owen's head jerked up. "We

WATCH SECTIONS

A submarine must be battle-ready and maneuverable twenty-four hours a day. Duty shifts were 8–12, 12–4 and 4–8. Someone on, for example, the 12–4 watch would be on duty in the afternoon and also the middle of the night. When a battle was immanent, men not on their regular watch also had special assigned duty stations.

ain't hooked up yet for drinking. But you don't never pull away like that. Fresh water's precious, and we need the drips from when yer done for washing dishes."

"Didn't know that," murmured Owen. He wondered if he should explain and apologize some more—to tell Smitty he'd never actually finished sub school so didn't know everything.

Smitty looked Owen over again. "Maybe you do look like a kid. Well, I suppose I look like a grandpa to you. But you do your baking and I do my cooking, and we'll get on just fine." He grinned. "But I ain't an old grandpa. I can make a pretty good fist. So any of the fellows gives you a rough time about being, well—sorta what you could call 'younger,' you see me. Or better yet—bake up some doughnuts, then spit in 'em. A navy man's a navy man, far as I'm concerned."

He held out an arm festooned with anchor and heart tattoos. Smitty's hand pressed hard into Owen's. A solid shake. A welcome. Owen's second on the *Mako*.

Smitty was grinning a toothy grin as he continued. "You and me, Owen, we're pretty much what you'd call unique on the *Mako*. The others all got assigned watch sections: there's the 8to12s, the 12to4s and the 4to8s. They stick together. But you and me—we're loners. We don't belong to any watch section. We work by our lonesomes."

Owen stared at Smitty. He never quite put it together that way before.

A loner isn't what Owen had signed up to be.

L O C A T I O N: Manitowoc, Wisconsin.
Lake Michigan
Enrique Romero
First Dive

Enrique stroked the bronze nose of number twenty-four torpedo, the last to be loaded. Now the *Mako* was armed and dangerous. A lethal machine. Just like he wanted it to be.

He heard the intercom click on above his head. A little black circle hidden in the tangle of pipes and cords on the sub's ceiling was their lifeline connecting the whole boat.

"Attention. This is the captain speaking. It's time to put the *Mako* through her paces. The depth here is right for our first full test dive. Proceed to your stations. Captain out."

"Nicky! Let's get going!" Enrique grabbed Nick by his denim collar, and lunged from the forward torpedo room toward the control room.

"I'm coming, I'm coming," gasped Nick, pushing with Enrique against the tide of the other sailors rushing through the narrow corridor.

Enrique and Nick would control the flippers—or "planes"—mounted on the front and back ends of the submarine. Like a dolphin, they guided angle and depth of the boat underwater. Enrique sat down on the stool next to Nick's.

Planesmen on bow and stern planes

The officers stood behind them in the control room, issuing orders.

"Engine off."

"Engine off, aye-aye." Everyone repeated things. There couldn't be any mistakes.

"Close vents."

"Close vents, aye-aye."

Enrique lifted his eyes to see Chief Miller pulling silver knobs from right to left, from "Rigged for Surface" to "Rigged for Diving." One light after another switched from red to green on the control panel called the "Christmas Tree."

"Green board, we've got pressure in the boat, Captain."

"Understood. Dive to seventy feet."

"Seventy feet, aye-aye."

THE LIVING SUBMARINE

All the parts of the boat are interconnected, as in a living body. Propulsion control is primarily toward the rear, and batteries are both forward and aft. Fuel and ballast (water/air) tanks run most of its length. The conning tower might be thought of as the brain, or nerve center, of the submarine, the place from which battles are directed. Right below it is the control room, which regulates diving. Strategy sessions, decoding of messages, reading maps and charts, as well as sleeping and relaxing, take place in the officers' wardroom. Every part of the boat has multiple uses to support the functions of the whole.

"Seventy feet, aye-aye."

Mr. Anderson reached up to twist the dial that blasted out the diving alarm: "AhOOOHgah! AhOOOHgah!"

Enrique felt an electric thrill in his body. His first dive was starting. They were going under the water—far deeper than he'd ever swum.

"Open tanks."

"Open tanks!" Chief Miller threw the levers by his feet. Air whooshed out from the storage tanks. Water roared in, weighing down the boat. A thunderous sound boomed from the deck and bulkheads and all around the hull—a sound that vibrated up from Enrique's feet clear through his fingertips.

Enrique and Nick were synchronized with their wheels and dials, just like at sub school. Nick did angle and Enrique did speed to get down to the ordered seventy feet. Enrique kept his eyes on the huge, clocklike gauge. But suddenly the dial started spinning too fast. He gripped the wheel with all his strength to slow it down.

"Taper off, Romero!" came Mr. Anderson's sharp voice.

"I can't hold it, sir!"

In the same moment there was a tremendous clatter and a sound of something ricocheting off metal, then a *whooopa-whoopa-whoopa* rolling sound. All the lights in the control room went out.

Enrique couldn't have said what he was aware of first, since everything was happening all at once. He felt a quick, bruising pain in his right foot. Instinctively, he reached down to touch the thing that hit him. It was a can.

Emergency power flickered on. The light showed three big cans of peaches strewn around the control room floor. Peaches.

CHIEF OF THE BOAT

Ranked between the "ordinary" enlisted man and the officers are several "chiefs." The Chief of the Boat (C.O.B.) is in charge of assigning bunks, disciplining crewmen, supervising water use, scheduling haircuts, changes in the watch list and assigning cleaning duties. His battle station is the "Christmas Tree," operating the hydraulic (water powered) manifold of levers to the ballast tank vents and positive buoyancy vents for diving and surfacing. In preparing to dive, vents show red when open and green when closed.

HOW A SUBMARINE WORKS

A submarine takes in seawater, or pumps it out, to sink or float. It dives by opening tanks to let in water. Below the surface it uses the bow planes (a pair of broad, horizontal "flippers") at the front of the boat, and stern planes (smaller "fins") at the rear to maneuver, while shifting varying quantities of water between the tanks. Because air is much lighter than water, when the sub surfaces, air under great pressure is let into the tanks, forcing the water out.

Canned peaches, of all things, had made them go dark. Had wrecked the first dive.

Mr. Anderson glanced at Enrique and Nick, then quickly said, "Musta caused a short in the distribution panel when the can hit. Not the planeman's fault. Did anybody know about these cans? I didn't have them on my list when I made dive calculations."

Enrique held his breath to see what the skipper would say.

Captain Abbott grunted. "Blow the ballast tanks. Let's surface and try that dive again. And again and again, till it's right. Meantime, check the other compartments for loose supplies. And someone tell Pasquerly to use those cans quick—bake us a peach cobbler so we don't have them bouncing around the boat."

L O C A T I O N: Lake Michigan
Owen Pasquerly
Peach Cobbler

Just because it was cans of food that bounced out in the control room during the dive, the fellas kept staring at Smitty and Owen like it must be their fault. But Owen hadn't put any cans away. He'd seen Buzz Gretz with a crate of peaches. He was supposed to tell Mr. Anderson how much they weighed and where he'd put them, so the submarine could be balanced. If not, it could mess up a dive. Which is what had happened. Which is why Owen had to bake peach cobbler. Captain's orders.

He'd never baked anything on the *Mako*. Now he had to bake something he'd never made before, in an oven he'd never used. And he had to please the captain. All because someone else had messed up.

Owen set the three giant cans of peaches on the galley counter with a thunk. Then he lifted them and thunked them down harder.

"You got a recipe for peach cobbler in yer baker's handbook?"

Smitty had appeared, his bulky frame wedged sideways in the galley's door.

"Yeah," said Owen. "Never made it before, so it could taste like yellow turds and glue for all I know."

"Well, yer on yer own. But least ways, I brought some flour and baking powder and sugar. Suppose it's easier than starting with bread. So that's the bright side." Smitty thumped Owen on the back. Owen's lungs lurched. "I'm gettin' me some shut-eye. See you in the a.m."

Owen was alone now. He whapped the bottom of a flour bag, catapulting flour into the mixing bowl. A cloud of white dust rose up, choking him. Fun night this is going to be, Owen fumed. *On top of the rest of the fun I'm having.*

The galley

During the dive, he and Smitty were assigned to the galley and mess. Big deal. They got to close a ventilation duct. And be sure no cookie sheets or pots clanged around. That was their battle station, too. Like being around an oven and tables and chairs during battle was something exciting.

Nick and Enrique got to be in the control room, or up topside. They had a real job. They did lookout. They guided the wheels to the bow and stern planes. They were part of the diving team. Owen wasn't part of any team.

Owen yanked the measuring cups off their hooks. That's what he got to work with. Not torpedoes. Not gauges. Not the helm or the periscope. *Where's the glory in baking bread?*

He read his recipe. Added one dumb ingredient after the other. Split the batter into three parts to bake three times. Stupid tiny oven.

The *Mako* hadn't even left stateside, and already Owen knew this wasn't turning out right.

L O C A T I O N: New Orleans Harbor and
the Gulf of Mexico
Nick Gallagher
First Taste of Salt

The *Mako* was decked out in banners and flags. She'd been
floated on a barge down the Mississippi River, and now sat
bobbing in the New Orleans harbor, waiting to set out to sea.
The mayor just finished making a speech, and a band started
playing march music.

On the pier, Nick watched as the man who looked just like
Enrique, except with gray hair, waved his hands to sweep
all the guys together to fit into a picture. Enrique's dad and
brother had come on the bus from California to say good-bye.
Nick wished his own dad or mom had been able to come to
see him off, but of course that would not happen. They didn't
have the money to spend on a ticket from Minnesota to New
Orleans. Anyway, how could they leave the work and the
animals on the farm?

Nick felt squished between Enrique and the other guys.
There was Tom Benson, who looked smart as a college professor
and parted his hair down the middle. Skinny Eddie Haverly,
who always wanted to be on top of any news. "Doc" Davis,

who planned on being a doctor someday. Eric Edison, who had more submarine experience than any of them. "Sparks" Huot, who operated the ship's radio. And Enrique.

The flash from the camera must have messed up his eyes, because Nick could have sworn, looking out over the crowd after the picture taking stopped, that he saw his mom. Mom, tall and lean, her feet firmly planted. He saw how her hand came to her throat, fingers fluttering around it as she did when she worried. Then she waved, right at him, in the stiff way she had.

It couldn't be her. It *was* her.

"Mom! Mom! . . . You . . . Mom!" was all Nick could say, as they opened their arms to each other. They weren't used to a lot of hugs, so after a few moments they pulled back. "How did you manage . . . to get here . . . had to have been real expensive," he said, stammering.

"My hens have been laying well. I used my egg money." Nick could barely hear her voice over the noise of the band and the crowd. "Your father and I decided it would give you heart to see a wave. As you . . . leave . . . going so far away . . ." Nick saw his mother's hand come again to her throat.

She sniffed. "Introduce me to your friends, won't you, son?" She listened to all the names, to where they were from, and asked them about their duties.

"Who is that boy, Nick, off by himself?" she asked, looking past a cluster of noisy sailors and families.

"Oh, he's the baker. A new guy. Joined us right before we left Manitowoc."

"Doesn't he have any family here, or friends?"

"I don't know. Maybe not."

"I'd like to meet him. Take me over there, will you?"

Nick held his mother's elbow in his palm. It felt bony and familiar, a shape like his own. They couldn't move fast through the crowd, and that was fine with Nick. He didn't want to be mushy; he just wanted to be there with her for the time that was left. He guided her past sailors kissing their crying girlfriends and mothers. Past the captain, who lifted up his wife and baby and swung them around. A bearded old man shook hands with Smitty. A little girl clung to Mr. Anderson's leg. "Don't leave me, Pauly! Don't go!"

After all the pairs of people crying and hugging and kissing, Nick saw Owen. His red hair was standing up straight as a bristle brush. He kept spinning around in a little circle. He reminded Nick of a calf by itself out in a field.

Maybe he'd look out for Owen.

"Uh—Pasquerly. This is my mom."

Owen stopped spinning.

"And what's his first name, Nick? Mind your manners."

"Oh, yeah. His name's Owen."

"How do you do, Mrs. Gallagher?" asked Owen.

"I do just fine. This is a big day for you."

"Suppose it is," replied Owen.

"Where do you come from, Owen?"

"Montana. Western Montana. Town called Missoula."

"Such a beautiful part of the country. We have no mountains where we come from, in Minnesota. And your family. They'll surely miss you."

"Well, they . . . I don't think so."

She paused. "I hope you'll let me . . . thank you . . . for serving your country."

"Well, I'm just baking is all. That's what they want me to do." Owen stared at his shoes.

"That's serving, too. I wonder. When I write letters to Nick, would you like me to write you, too? Just little newsy cards."

"We can't get mail out at sea, Mom," said Nick. He'd told her that before. She'd seemed nervous and forgetful ever since he'd decided to go to war.

"I can send them to Australia. You go on leave there, don't you?"

"That's right, Mom. And then we can send mail back stateside."

A noisy stream of sailors sprinted from land onto the deck of the submarine. "Over there! Over there! Oh, the Yanks are coming, the Yanks are here . . ." Nick's feet twitched to the rousing sound of the patriotic songs the band was playing. He wanted to pull away from her now.

"We need to go now, Mom. This is it."

Her eyes got wide. "Nick . . . I—" But Owen interrupted. Nick was glad.

"Thanks for, I mean, it was good to meet you."

Mrs. Gallagher held out her hand to shake Owen's. She held his hand an extra moment and patted it like mothers do. "And—I'd like some letters. That'd be swell," said Owen, turning away and jumping onto the dock and the submarine. She watched him join in with the other sailors before turning back to Nick.

"It was the right thing to do, Mom. I mean, for you to sign the papers, so I could join up. I'll learn things. I'll be more help on the farm . . ." Nick talked fast. He didn't want her to cry.

"I know, Nick. You're seventeen now. Time you made your

own decisions." Again her hand fluttered at her throat. Then Nick's arms were around her back, and he felt a breath drawn in. It wasn't quite a sob, or a word. He didn't know if it was in his chest or hers. Then his heart and eardrums ripped apart with the wonderful call of the submarine's klaxon.

AhOOOOgah! AhOOOOgah!

"It's the diving alarm. I guess it means . . . I really have to go." Nick squeezed her shoulder, then pulled away, letting himself be swept with the other sailors onto the submarine.

Nick wasn't sure if it was by accident, or if Owen had decided to stand next to him on deck. "We're off to sea!" Owen squealed.

The moorings were sliced and the *Mako* bounced and swayed on the waters below their feet. They were going. Finally. Tugboats pulled the *Mako* out of the harbor before Chief Itty and his motor macs revved up her engines.

With each sway up, then down, Nick breathed more strongly the scent of sea air. He had an urge to lick his lips. Salt. The taste of the sea.

"Boy, they sure look little, don't they?" asked Owen. Nick didn't answer. He just watched the waving families onshore becoming little dots in the distance. He couldn't tell which dot was Mom.

Would it seem short, or like forever, before he would again see ripe corn in a field? Or the barn on the hill and Mom in her kitchen?

But now Nick had a new world, and a new home. The *Mako:* the "fighting shark submarine." Her name said what she was all about: a fighter. He'd do some fighting. Have adventures. Be with friends that he would never have met in Minnesota.

Enrique had come over to stand with him and Owen, and so had Eddie, Sparks, Tom, Doc, and Eric. They were all together. Behind them was land: solid and known. The blue water, though—Nick sniffed it in again—that was a blank, waiting for them, pulling them out. Out to sea.

L O C A T I O N: Atlantic Ocean, Forward
Torpedo Room of the Mako
Owen Pasquerly
Bunking with Torpedoes

Owen lay dozing, swayed gently between trees that smelled like—oil. *Are trees supposed to smell like that?* he wondered groggily. Gradually, he became aware of the vinyl mattress cover under his palms. The *Mako* was rocking him. Trees were back home. The rich, heavy scent of the engines' fuel lined his nostrils.

Owen felt a drip from overhead. The torpedo suspended above his bunk, huge and heavy, was sweating from the heat. He wiped the splash off his face and was nearly asleep again when he heard voices half-whispering. It was Nick and Enrique, from on top of their torpedoes.

"Hey there, Nicky. What's up?"

"Nothin'. Just thinkin'. Go to sleep."

"Can't sleep. Too excited. My brain's jumping. Let's talk."

"About what?"

"About anything. Just talk. Say, what do you think about the baker fella?"

Bunking in the forward torpedo room

Owen closed his eyes tighter so they wouldn't notice he was awake.

"What do you mean, 'what do I think?' "

"Well, he's—wait. Let me check."

Owen heard the soft clink and groan of the chains holding the upper bunks, and knew Enrique had swiveled around to look down at him. He lay still.

"OK. He's sleeping like a baby."

"He is a baby. He's too short and scrawny to be seventeen. Gotta have lied and snuck in."

"Hey! How about me? Some people are just naturally short."

"Naw. I've been around animals all my life. And people are animals, too. That guy's like a calf. Not near full grown."

DEADLY GIANTS

A submarine leaves port with twenty-four torpedoes, each of them about twenty feet long. Each has a warhead at its tip and complicated inner workings to propel it. Four are sealed up and ready to go in the after torpedo room tubes and six in the forward torpedo room's tubes. The other fourteen are placed on racks. The crew assigned to torpedo rooms must sleep over, under, or next to the torpedoes. As battles are fought, the spares are gradually loaded into the tubes and launched, leaving more space inside the torpedo rooms.

"Yeah. He seems different. Younger, I guess. Are you going to turn him in?"

Owen stiffened, but didn't stir.

"Why would I do that? He's an all right fella. Besides, my mom liked him."

Owen breathed again. He became aware of the funny *wheewheewhee* snores of Tom Benson, and the little suction sounds as guys shifted in their sleep on their mattress covers. No sheets on a submarine. No way to wash them.

Enrique spoke again, his half-whisper voice sounding tense. "Hey, Nicky. Lotta ammo in these fish, eh?"

"Yeah."

"You know some of 'em might be duds? Happened on the *Urchin* and the *Orca*. Other boats, too. Captain says, 'Fire!' and—*pfflaat*. Nothin'."

" 'Course, I know that," replied Nick, grumpily.

"Japs don't know we're close by till we fire the torpedoes. Then we got a dud and they come back at us, mad as a bull. Those tankers and transport ships—they're way bigger than we are."

"Don't think about it. Go to sleep. Gotta be up again before midnight."

Enrique sighed. "Yeah. 'Night, Nicky."

Owen finally drifted off again, dreaming of a hammock and trees. He was back home, in Montana. But the war was on. Pop was gunning for him. And all he had was a dud torpedo.

L O C A T I O N: Atlantic Ocean, Nighttime
on the Mako
Owen Pasquerly
Seventeen Loaves of Bread

Sliding, shuffling sounds stirred Owen's sleep. Was Ma in her slippers, out in the hallway? Then he heard a clunking noise and jolted up, hitting his knee on the torpedo above him. He was on the submarine. Owen blinked his eyes, shook his head, and held his arm out to get enough glow from the ceiling light to read his watch: 11:41 p.m.

A leg descending from the torpedo above him mushed down the edge of his mattress. It was Eddie Haverly. "Oops. Sorry, Pasquerly," he said. Owen's arm knocked against Nick, as he and Enrique were buckling their sandals and putting on their sailor caps and jackets. They were getting ready to go topside. They were wearing goggles with red lenses.

"What are those things for? You guys look like you're from Mars," said Owen.

"Shh." Nick's finger came up to his nosepiece. It made his goggle eyes look even stranger.

"Yeah," added Enrique in a low voice. "Not everybody in here's on 12to4s. We gotta wear the goggles before watch. To get our eyes set for seeing at night."

"Remember you have to get up soon, too," said Nick. "Other guys need our bunks."

"I know, I know. You don't have to tell me everything," said Owen. Since it was his first night for baking bread, Mr. Anderson had said Owen could get some extra sleep. But from tomorrow on, he'd need to start baking by eight or nine at night, after Smitty finished cooking dinner.

Like the rest of the guys, Owen had slept in his underwear. He pulled on his dungarees and slapped on his sandals so he could walk with Enrique and Nick.

Owen felt the *GGgggrrrrrrhhhmmmm* of the *Mako*'s engines vibrating through his guts. It was the sound that the submarine made on the surface, charging up her immense batteries. He liked the sound. It felt like it was charging him up, too. They wound their way through narrow corridors from the forward torpedo room, past the curtained doorways where the skipper and officers were sleeping, to the control room. Enrique and Nick stopped.

The control room was just below the conning tower and the bridge, topside. It was lit in red light, making all the dials and wheels look weird. Owen figured he couldn't ever learn to operate that stuff.

Nick reached behind his head to unfasten the goggles, muttering as it caught on one of his ears. Enrique laughed and grabbed at his friend's big ear, flapping it back and forth. Nick whacked him—"Get off it, Romeo—" then stepped up the ladder to the bridge.

"Adios—bake us something good," said Enrique, turning to grin at Owen as he climbed up the ladder.

Did saying "adios" mean Enrique considered him a buddy? "Romeo" was different. Pop would've called him a "spic." What was a spic, anyway? Must be some kind of a bad name. Probably Enrique wouldn't like being called it, whatever it was.

Owen kept going to the radio room, then the galley.

"Are you Pasquerly?" asked a sleepy voice behind him. Owen turned to see a round-faced, pudgy sailor a little taller than himself.

"That's me."

"I'm Al Kaluza," he sniffed. "I'm supposed to help you, but I don't know nothin' about baking."

Back home, whenever they needed to hire extra help to bake for a wedding or holiday, it was always Pop who was in charge. Now Owen was in charge. How was he going to do that?

"Well, I know about baking, so I guess I'm your boss," Owen replied, folding his arms, trying to look important.

"My boss?" Kaluza's lip puffed out. "You ain't an officer."

Owen wasn't sure what to say. Pop was the boss he knew about. Bosses bossed people around.

"If you're helping, that means I'm the boss." Owen tried to say "means" sternly, but his voice squeaked.

Kaluza rubbed his face and yawned. "How about you just tell me what needs doing and we'll be partners?"

"OK," said Owen.

"So what do we do first?"

Owen tried to sound sure about what to do. "We get the flour and the yeast and everything we need."

That made sense. Owen liked the sound of what he'd just said.

"Where is all that stuff?"

In his brain, Smitty's booming voice came again: "Flour's in blahblahblah, eggs are blahblahblah." But what had Smitty really said? So much had happened since he arrived on the *Mako*. Bread baking was the one thing Owen was supposed to be good at. What if he couldn't even get started? Why had Mr. Anderson let him wait till midnight to begin, anyway?

Owen wanted to say, "Let's just forget it and go back to bed," but he was in the Navy. He'd wanted to be in the middle of this war and not stuck in a little bakery. Now here he was.

Owen started opening cupboards and drawers. The flour bin was next to the oven. It swung open into Owen's hand to offer up only a few handfuls of flour on the bottom of the bin. He had to think where the rest would be. Can't make bread without flour.

"You suppose the flour sacks are down below?" asked Kaluza.

"Yeah! Right!" That's what Smitty had said. But those bags would be awfully heavy.

"I'll go," said Kaluza, squatting down to pull the square handle notched into the floor. A narrow ladder led straight down into the cool, dark hole crammed with supplies.

Owen swiveled on his sandals, back into the galley. *Where's the salt? That's pepper. Don't need it. Sugar. Need that. Salt. Over the stove. OK. Yeast. Bread won't rise without yeast. Here? No. Dang it! What's that? This isn't how we store stuff at home. In that can? Yup. All right. Smitty told me. What. Eggs. Eggs. In the escape hatch?*

Owen reminded himself he was a baker. A baker's boy, anyway. He could do this. He did it all the time at home. It was just different here. He splashed warm water onto his wrist. He knew the right feel of the water to coax the yeast and make the bread rise. While Kaluza fetched the eggs, Owen slit open the first bag of flour and poured the soft powder into the mixing bowl. He breathed the scents of yeast, of powder rising in a poof from the bowl.

He peered into the tiny oven. Did it have to be that small? Only four loaves would fit at a time, no matter how he fiddled with the bread pans. It would take five batches: five times of repeating all the steps of pouring, mixing, punching the dough, rising and baking. Seventeen loaves he needed. He'd have to work fast. He'd have three loaves to spare in case he messed up.

Mixing he could handle. But lots can go wrong in baking. He hadn't cared if the peach cobbler turned out because it wasn't fair that he had to make it. But bread: that was his job. Bread was the only reason they let him be here.

Five batches. Five chances to get it wrong.

L O C A T I O N: Atlantic Ocean, Topside
the Mako
Nick Gallagher
"Right Full Rudder"

"Reporting for watch duty, Mr. Anderson," said Nick, standing topside at the *Mako*'s hatch. The cool night air flew into his nostrils like a blast of energy. The open sea reminded Nick of rolling, unending cornfields at home. Nick and Enrique would be partners on watch. This was more or less just practice. They were still too close to the U.S. to encounter the enemy. Probably.

"Welcome to your first night. You'll be on lookout, relieving each other every twenty minutes," said Mr. Anderson. "Remember that. Twenty minutes. We can't afford eyestrain. The last 8to12s are waiting for you."

Nick could feel Enrique next to him, quivering with excitement. Enrique started clicking his fingers and slapping his thighs like he did when he had too much energy.

Nick climbed up to his lookout perch, tapped the 8to12 on the shoulder for his binoculars, then swung the cord around his neck. A metal hoop surrounded his waist to steady him when the waves swelled suddenly. It felt cool and smooth when he bumped against it. His duty was to scan sea and sky, looking just above the horizon line. The binocs were heavy and clunky and made little press marks around his eyes.

Lookout

Green, glittery patches floated on the water, like melted fireworks. *What would it feel like to touch?* wondered Nick. He'd heard about it at sub school, but didn't know it would look so pretty. The glow was caused by colonies of little water animals.

Tom Benson tapped him to signal his twenty minutes

was up. He went below with Enrique for a stretch break and snack, then came up again to scan. Then stretch break and scan again. It was getting to be a rhythm. What had Mr. Anderson said about not getting too comfortable? Nick couldn't quite remember.

The melted fireworks on the water parted in the distance, like a long furrow line in a field. *What's that?* Nick wondered, a cold feeling suddenly curling through his guts. Then he knew.

Torpedoes! A pair of them, streaking toward the *Mako!*

If the sub didn't swerve, they'd be rammed and sink to the bottom of the sea. Nick's voice wadded up like a cotton ball in his chest. "Ri . . . i . . ." he stammered, then strangled out the words: "Right . . . Full . . . Rudder!" But was it loud enough to be heard over the noise of the engines?

Mr. Anderson swung around and stared up at Nick.

In the next instant, the boat heaved to one side. There was shouting. Guys running. Then the lightning-fast, torpedo-shaped forms swerved and slowed to arc up and play in the waves off the submarine's bow. Not torpedoes. Dolphins.

They grinned their mysterious dolphin grins, swiveling on their sides to peer up at the submariners.

Nick panted from the energy it took to sound the alarm. He gulped. *Stupid idiot. Dolphins!*

Enrique was laughing so hard he nearly fell from the lookout perch. Nick scowled at him and muttered, "Well, you're the big deal torpedo man, not me."

From the bridge came the voice of Mr. Anderson. He was only a little older than Nick, but right now he sounded stern and strong: like he really should be called "mister."

"Knock off the ha-ha's. I told you guys before: any doubts about what you see, you speak up." There was silence.

Turning to Enrique, he asked, "When did you spot them? Exactly."

Enrique looked alarmed. "Well, sir—soon as I heard Gallagher, I swung around and scanned with my binocs. But it's awfully dark, so I didn't see anything right away. Guess it could've been thirty seconds."

"Thirty seconds. We aren't the only ones with submarines. Could have been the Japs, or—out here—the Germans. If they had been torpedoes, thirty seconds' warning and we might have ducked them. Thirty seconds between waking up to another day, and being blown to kingdom come."

Mr. Anderson turned to look hard and wonderingly at Nick.

"Those are some peepers you've got. Ever had your night vision tested?"

"No, sir. I mean—they checked me at sub school, but a dark room's different from being outside."

"Well, it got tested tonight."

"It's that living way out in the country—he's never seen city lights to wreck his eyes," said Enrique.

"That right?"

"I don't know if it's from being on the farm, but people have always told me they can't see as clear at night as I can."

A grin spread across Mr. Anderson's lean face.

"Well, now. I'm thinking the 12to4s have a prize lookout. We might need you for some special assignments. Now take a break."

Nick wasn't used to compliments. Still. He *did* spot what

nobody else did. But what a dumb mistake. He walked slowly, shuffling his feet and staring down at the deck.

"You know, Gallagher," said Mr. Anderson, following him, "those eyes of yours—I've got a feeling you're going to make this war patrol a success."

"Yes, sir," replied Nick. "If I can learn to tell a torpedo from a dolphin."

Mr. Anderson was depending on him to see things on watch. But what if next time he didn't see, and they really were torpedoes?

Batch number one. Bread burned. Just a little.

Batch number two. Bread perfect. Dumb luck. Can I do it again?

Batch number three. Bread lopsided. How can anybody be expected to bake perfect bread when waves bounce the sub up and down?

Batch number four. Bread rose too high. Going to have big holes inside. Outside looks OK. Maybe I get away with it.

Batch number five. Who knows? In the oven. Could wreck everything.

Owen carefully stacked his steaming bread loaves on two tables in the mess. He'd save the best loaves for the captain and officers.

Why the eating area—which was also the main lounging spot on the boat—was called a "mess," Owen didn't know. It wasn't messy, even though it was small. He sat cross-legged on a bench. The engines' growly hum mixed with the water's swooshing sounds around the boat. Probably they'd be submerging soon, with daylight coming on. Owen liked diving.

He was tired and wanted to go back to bed. When the last batch finished he would. Now he had to study. The others had learned all this stuff in submarine school; he'd been in a quick course because they needed bakers. How about that, anyway? Baking: to him the most ordinary thing in the world. So he was turning out to be a baker. Like Pop.

Pop said schooling was for uppity folks. Back home, Owen was careful if there were high grades on his report card to show it just to Ma. She wouldn't say anything out loud in case Pop heard her, but she'd pat Owen on the arm and be smiling for a long time afterward. If Pop knew about something good Owen did in school, he'd snarl, "Trying to show up your old man, ya runt kid?"

But Captain Abbott seemed just the opposite of Pop. At least about studying. Owen had to get at least pretty good at knowing the whole submarine: it was the captain's orders, back on that first day they met. But would he learn enough to satisfy the captain? And why wasn't bread baking enough? It was plenty hard. Just let any of the other guys try it and they'd find out.

The main book for him to know was *The Fleet Submarine: Design and Operation Specifications*. When he found something he'd need to remember, he drew a star next to it and wrote "Important" in neat letters in the margin. He had to know the difference between the hydraulic manifold and the trim manifold, and how the ovens in the galley got their heat and thousands of other things. He flipped back through the pages he'd read to see if he'd done enough for now. But there were stars and "Important" marks on almost every page. How could he learn all this? Was the captain really going to test him on it? Owen rubbed his eyes. *Does Gary have to study this much, being a flyer?*

He tossed the book over his racks of bread onto a bench, stood, and twisted all around as he yawned and stretched. He didn't even graze the pipes and wires that crisscrossed the ceiling.

Pop hated having a son as small as Owen, but the sub was the perfect size for him: small and compact. It fit close around him, and he already knew how to move in it. *Funny how there's so much more space at the bakery, but I feel hemmed in there and not here.* Owen realized with a jolt that it was because, after Pop turned mean a couple of years ago, he was always jumpy at home about what Pop might do next.

Time for a head stop. Owen sauntered down the corridor through the red-lit crew's quarters, past snoring and sleepy sailors, to the bathroom. After doing his business, he stood in the narrow head—that's what they called it on the submarine and Owen wanted to be sure to use the right words for things— looking straight down. *Long wooden lever—push with my left knee now . . . twist the knob—right hand . . . shove the high-up left lever in . . . Whoosh kathunkkathunk* noises told him he got it right. Not like the first time, when he'd gone "number two" and got it back on his face and spattered on his clothes. There wasn't a sink in the bathroom to wash it off, so the guys knew what had happened when he walked out. Buzz Gretz saw him and said, "Pee-eeeuwww. Got your baby poop all over your little baby uniform, eh?"

At least Buzz didn't bunk up in the forward torpedo room.

When Owen got back to the mess, he saw someone leaning over, sniffing his bread, poking a finger at a crispy corner of one of the loaves. One of the perfect loaves he had picked out for the officers. It was Enrique.

"Hey!" said Owen. "I'm saving that!"

Enrique reached just like the Mexican boy who came once to the bakery at home. Pop had whispered a cuss word that Owen didn't understand, just loud enough so the boy's mom heard and yanked him back. *Mexican. Spic.*

But Owen liked Enrique. Pop wouldn't be happy about that.

"How about we grab a stick of butter and slice this one open!" said Enrique,

"I guess since you poked it, you can eat it," muttered Owen, trying to decide which officer would be least mad if he got a not-perfect loaf.

Enrique chomped on the bread. "Ohhhhh. How'd you learn to bake like this?" Enrique was admiring his work. Owen decided he could spare the loaf.

Owen took his place again and sat cross-legged. "My pop taught me." *Before he turned mean and got drunk all the time,* added Owen to himself. Being out here, heading to sea and far from home—he wanted to tell Enrique. He missed Gary and needed friends. *But maybe he'll blab. And why was he wondering about me last night?* He liked Enrique, but wasn't ready to tell him a lot yet. Things like how Pop wanted to join up for the war, but his hearing was going bad, so they wouldn't take him. Pop said the Navy would get what they deserved when they took his runt kid son. The words felt like a slug in the stomach.

He saw Enrique looking quizzically at him, holding a chunk of steaming hot bread slathered with butter. Enrique lifted it up toward Owen's mouth. "C'mon now, Owen. Don't be moody. Open up. Gotta taste this with me."

It felt good to see Enrique grinning and wanting to share the bread with him. He asked sheepishly, "They call you Romeo, don't they?"

"'Course they do! For all my girlfriends."

"So why did you leave home? Why'd you join up for submarines?"

Enrique beamed. "Torpedoes! Where else could I shoot those beauties? If I'd waited to turn eighteen, I'd get drafted. They'd probably have stuck me in the army like a lot of us, even though I'm Angeleno. I wanted the Navy. To shoot big torpedoes at the Japs. And I didn't want to have to shave off my mustache."

"What mustache? You don't have a mustache."

"The one I'm *going* to have. You can on a submarine. Not like on other ships. I got two mustache combs for going-away presents, to keep it looking good. One from Nanette and this little silver one from Esperanza. Maybe I should use one comb on one side and one on the other so my girls don't get jealous?" He winked at Owen. Owen just had a little fuzz on his face. He couldn't have grown a mustache for anything. Owen hated it when he blushed, but he felt the pink spreading across his freckled face and said, "I better get back to my studying." "Anything you want to know about subs, or you forget anything—you just ask me. Or anything about girls—I'm the man to help you out," said Enrique, pointing at his chest with his thumb. He took his hunk of buttery bread and walked out of the mess.

Enrique wasn't anything like Gary, but he'd told Owen he'd help him.

What would happen with him and Enrique Romero?

Yikes! Batch number five. Not going to be perfect.

L O C A T I O N: Classified Information:
Undisclosed Pacific Locale
Enrique Romero
Seasick

Enrique felt lucky to be a lookout. Lookouts get topside to fresh
sea air. His mustache was growing in. He raised his free arm
to smooth the hairs down. He was standing lookout now, with
Nick and Eric.

He was supposed to watch only the tips of the waves. They
were slate gray: higher than usual, with white caps. Enrique
couldn't resist tipping his binoculars up to view the afternoon
sky. Rippled gray-green clouds streaked ominously across the
sun. Thunder rumbled like a growling dog.

They weren't supposed to talk on lookout, but finally Enrique
couldn't stand it any longer. "You think maybe the weather's
trying to tell us something?" he hollered up to Nick, who was
in the crow's nest.

"Weather tells us all kinds of things," Nick shouted back,
over the whistling, gusting wind. "I'm thinking we'd better pay
attention to it now."

A deafening clap of thunder jolted Nick on his narrow
platform, nearly pitching him overboard. Nick grabbed for the

rope and metal clips clanging in the wind to strap himself in place. Lightning forked across the sky like a bony hand. "C'mon down from there, Gallagher," yelled Mr. Anderson. "Let's not get you electrocuted."

A huge wave washed over the deck and onto the bridge. Enrique found himself sprawled on the deck, tangled up with Eric and Mr. Anderson. They'd knocked each other over like bowling pins. "Geez! Did you see that wave?" gasped Eric, his eyes popping and mouth dropping open. Enrique started to laugh at Eric, and at how they all must look with their drenched hair and sopping clothes, elbows and knees pointing every which way.

Nick wobbled down the rungs of the slippery bridge ladder, as the other three struggled to their feet.

"Keep your binocs up—I'm going to see about continuing the watch from inside the conning tower," hollered Mr. Anderson.

Enrique, Nick, and Eric pushed their backs into the spray shield on the bridge. It helped keep their footing in the wind. Enrique rubbed his sleeve on the binoculars, but they kept getting so speckled with rain and sea spray they were almost worthless. He wanted to say something to the others—to grumble about having to stay at their posts during such a storm—but he'd already talked once on lookout today and better not again.

Mr. Anderson yanked on Enrique's arm to get his attention, and pointed: *Down! Down!*

First Eric, then Enrique, then Nick slid through the conning tower hatch, followed by Mr. Anderson, who reached up to dog the hatch. Captain Abbott was in the conning tower, talking with Mr. Zelks.

"It's just kind of unpleasant now, but soon it won't be possible to stand watch on the bridge," said Mr. Zelks, "or you'll get washed overboard. So, Cap'n wants to show you how to do lookout through the periscope."

The periscope! A thrilled shiver cascaded down Enrique's body, on top of his shivers from wet clothes. *Only officers get to look through the periscope!*

Enrique, Nick, and Eric clustered around Captain Abbott in the crowded conning tower. Enrique sniffed in a smell of wet hair and skin, mixed with the normal sub smells of diesel oil and old sweat. "I'm not submerging, even though we're going to get a good tossing about," the captain explained. "Surface speed's much faster. We've got a schedule to keep to get to our base in Australia. These waves'll be higher than the boat soon: thirty, forty feet tall. Periscope can reach fifty feet. But you're going to feel a real yank on the scope when it gets slapped, so switch more often than your normal twenty minutes—those of you that can handle it, of course," he added.

Handle it? thought Enrique. *Of course we can handle it!* But there was a serious way in which the captain said it that made him unsure what he meant.

Enrique, Nick, and Eric took turns nudging their faces into the eyepiece. The captain adjusted their shoulders over the side levers so they could feel how to control the swivel of the periscope. Enrique had seen diagrams of the view through the periscope, with its notches for lining up a target before firing torpedoes. But the real thing felt dangerous and alive as it met his face and arms.

"I'll round up a bucket for the conning tower. And bring water up here," said Mr. Zelks.

"Good. Smitty's probably already on it, but make sure cans and buckets get set up throughout the boat," said the captain, as he lithely swung himself down the ladder from the conning tower to the control room. Mr. Zelks followed him, but with his rounder belly, he wasn't as agile as the captain.

Buckets? Cans? What for? wondered Enrique, but he was used to strange-sounding orders and didn't ask.

In the next hour, the storm became frenzied: shoving the *Mako* like a toy boat up to the tips of the towering waves, where it hovered an instant before being hurled nose down, submerging the bow completely. Seawater roared across the deck, sounding inside like hundreds of furiously pounding hammers. Then the boat would lurch up and level off before being slammed down again.

Enrique sat on the floor, to be most stable, as he looked through the scope. It vibrated into his chest, and swung crazily in the storm: he couldn't hold it still for long. Enrique's elbows were bruised from knocking into the instruments mounted on the bulkhead. Once his feet slid out from under him, and he couldn't help kicking Mr. Anderson.

Enrique heard Nick talking in a hoarse, quavering voice. "It's time for me to relieve you, Romeo, but . . . I'm not sure I—" He heard Nick make a retching, burping noise, then the splash of vomit hitting the tin bucket.

Enrique felt a vibration through his feet as Nick dropped into a heap on the conning tower's plate metal floor. Enrique pulled away from the scope. Mr. Anderson held Nick's shoulder, offering him a cup of water. Mr. Anderson's face—even his lips—had gone white. He was trembling like an old man in a nursing home.

Eric was at the helm. He grabbed for the bucket and got sick; Mr. Anderson reached behind him to grip the helm's huge wheel. *Is everybody going to get sick? How about me—am I, too? And who's going to control everything on this whole sub?* thought Enrique.

"Mr. Anderson," Enrique said, "do you want me to keep on the periscope, or should I take the helm. I've never done it before, but I guess I could."

"No . . . no . . . thanks. I can hang on awhile. You stay on the periscope. There's probably not a big chance the Japanese are out here—this far south—but captain wants us to keep lookouts as long as we can."

Enrique held on to the periscope until Owen tapped him on the shoulder.

"What are you doing here?" asked Enrique, knowing Owen wasn't a part of the watch section.

Owen grinned. "Just about all the guys down below are sick. I feel great. Captain asked did I think I could manage lookout, and I said sure."

"But you've never done lookout. Or handled the periscope."

"I can learn fast."

"We didn't use the periscope until today, either. Just show him," groaned Nick. "We could use a little help."

Owen shot a look of thanks Nick's way.

"Well, OK. You need to sit or kneel," began Enrique.

"That's not the right way to do it." Owen seemed afraid Enrique was kidding him.

"Not in the movies they don't, and not most times, but with the storm you do. This thing vibrates like a jackhammer on concrete, and it'll knock you over."

Enrique tipped Owen's jaw back and forth into position in the eyepiece. Then he draped Owen's arms over the side levers as if he were posing a store mannequin.

"Wow! This is great!" said Owen, his body jerking and spinning around the conning tower.

"You look like you're dancing for the first time. With a girl too tall for you," said Enrique.

"It's fun anyhow," said Owen. "And it's my turn, so you can go below for a while."

Enrique shrugged, then let himself slide down to the control room floor, not bothering with the rungs of the ladder. As he wove through the boat toward the forward torpedo room, Enrique saw slop buckets and tin cups every few feet. It smelled like vomit and dirty metal everywhere.

"They sure do spoil us in the submarine service," said Eddie, from up in his bunk. His voice was raspy. "Six meals a day— three down and three up."

"Crackers is what you need now," announced Smitty, plunking handfuls of soda crackers on every bunk as he bumped and banged his way through the lurching boat. "Crackers'll settle your stomach if anything can. Or anyhow—they ain't sharp and scratchy coming back up."

Sparks moaned from his bunk. "The whole world turns when I turn. I'm not eating or drinking anything!"

"Make yerself useful," said Smitty, motioning to Enrique to empty the sick buckets. Enrique's nose scrunched up, but he did it. Then he hurried back to the conning tower, where things were more interesting.

Nick sat in the corner holding his guts. Mr. Anderson was at the helm, and Owen was still at the periscope. "Can't hardly tell what's sea and what's sky out there," Owen said, stumbling as a fish slapped and shuddered against the lens. "Now I can't see nothin' at all."

Captain Abbott appeared at the top of the ladder. His odd, inscrutable eyes rested lightly a moment on Owen, and he gave a little grunt. Enrique didn't know if that meant he liked what he saw, or if Owen was in trouble. But the captain said: "Let's give it up. If there's an enemy out there, he'll be too busy fighting the storm to fight us."

Enrique's elbows and shoulders felt wobbly and sore. He walked to his bunk in the good old forward torpedo room.

The next day and the day after that were identical. Afternoon, midnight, and morning tumbled together, gray and sick smelling. The deck pitched and vibrated. Owen didn't do any baking; Smitty made soup for anyone who could eat. Enrique was tired into his bones from not sleeping and doing double watch duties to relieve fellows who couldn't get out of bed. He'd get thrown clear off his bunk from the lurching of the boat: off his mattress, over the torpedo, down past the lower bunk and slammed onto the narrow, hard floor. When he climbed back and started to doze, the boat would dip down into the waves and he'd jolt awake half way into another fall, his leg or head hanging out of his bunk.

Then the sullen sky eased into a vague, dreamy blue and the wind and waves calmed. First Sparks, then Nick, then Eddie and the others got out of their bunks. Smitty clattered around the galley again, making his chicken and corn fritters. The crackers and buckets were stowed away. Enrique and Owen were given extra time to catch up on sleep. But Enrique's eyes drowsily lifted when he heard the captain's voice over the intercom:

"All hands. This is the captain. We got a star reading at dawn, for the first time since the storm. We're a little off course but making good time. The Pacific has shown us her stuff. We'll pick up our orders shortly. So, look out, Japanese. Here comes the U.S.S. *Mako*."

L O C A T I O N: Undisclosed Pacific
Locale, En Route to Australia
Owen Pasquerly
Gingersnaps

"I used to like crackers, you know?" said Nick, crossing his sandaled foot over the mess bench. "But if I never eat one again, it'll be too soon."

"Me and Owen never stopped eating," said Enrique. "You guys being seasick left extra for us. 'Course—the menu was short on treats . . ." Enrique gave Owen a look.

Owen heaved a mock sigh. He liked being able to give the guys what they wanted—but he didn't want to seem too eager. He got up from his bench between Nick and Enrique and went into the galley. He opened a chrome cabinet, jostling tins of cinnamon, salt, parsley, and other seasonings. He had an idea, but he'd need to find ginger in here someplace. There. At the back. Its label was smudged, but he knew that sharp smell coming from around the shaking holes.

"If you guys help, I'll bake cookies."

"Deal," said Enrique.

"Just show me what to do," said Nick.

Owen was captain here. He sent Nick for flour, Enrique for

butter and eggs. They couldn't use the mixer as smoothly as he did. They didn't know anything about the magic of mixing powders and spices and oils together to make something great to eat. They took orders from Owen.

Aromas of ginger, cloves, and butter hovered in the air as Nick and Enrique spread the cookies out on cooling racks. It was crowded in the mess. They kept bumping into Al Kaluza and Billy Fedder, washing and stacking the dinner dishes. Owen was hanging up the measuring cups when he heard Captain Abbott's voice, cold and mean—not like Owen had ever heard him sound before.

"Clear the compartment. Everyone except Pasquerly. Now."

Al Kaluza dropped his dishrag. Nick said, "Aye, aye, Captain." Everyone shuffled out. Only Owen remained, facing the captain. He looked like Pop.

"Who told you about gingersnaps?" The green eyes glowed dangerously.

"Who . . . ah . . . well, ah, it was Ma taught me to make them . . ." stammered Owen.

"Don't think you can con me. It isn't going to make a difference. I'm not going easy on you about knowing the boat. So your special baking—gingersnaps. It's not counting for a thing."

"Not . . . counting?" asked Owen, clutching a cookie sheet to his chest like a shield and shrinking back. He knew this feeling from the bakery at home. He waited for a fist to come at him. But it didn't.

Captain Abbott stared at the cookie sheet, then at Owen's face, his eyes becoming just eyes again. He said: "The first day you came on board, I told you to study and learn the boat—

before we hit Australia. Well, we're nearly there. So—do you know your stuff?"

"Not all of it, Captain," replied Owen in a small voice. He felt confused and skinny, but the flare of fear had died down now that the skipper seemed calm.

"I'm going to ask you a few things. When we dive, do you prep the galley and mess, or does Smitty do it for you?"

"If I'm here by myself, I do it, Captain. I reach up to seal off the ventilation system's outboard valve. I can do that just fine."

"Good. And what would you do if you were walking through the control room and saw the planesman gripping the wheel?"

"Oh, I'd run over and grab his backside and pull, too. That would mean they'd lost hydraulic control of the bow or stern planes, and had to do it manually. And that's hard!"

Owen wasn't trying to be funny, but he saw on the captain's face that he was about to laugh. The crew sometimes called their captain "the Old Man." But this wasn't Pop.

Owen saw the captain look at the cookies.

"Just one more question about the boat. What do you do if we go to battle stations, gunnery?"

"Well, sir, I'm supposed to move aside the mess tables and hand up the ammo through the hatch. But—I'd like to be assigned to guns. I'm a pretty good shot."

"Is that right? I'll keep that in mind. But tell me. Of all the things you could have baked, why gingersnaps?"

"Well, Cap'n, after not baking so long, with the guys being seasick—it feels so good to . . . do my job again. And they were hinting around for snacks. I was going through the spices in the cupboard and saw this tin. It's ginger. Pop says cookies are too fussy for him, but Ma and me—that's what we like to make together. It made me . . . think of Ma."

"Well, your ma's good to think about. They make me think of my wife. She makes them when she wants to pamper me. I thought maybe someone told you about that. I overreacted. Smelling them made me . . . well . . ." He didn't finish, but instead reached for a cookie and bit down.

"You're a darn fine baker, you know that, sailor?" The captain lifted his ginger snap toward Owen.

Owen put the rack down. He reached for a cookie and took a bite, lifting his cookie, too.

The captain was the captain. Owen was the baker. They were both doing what they were good at. And that made them—in this regard, anyway—equals.

L O C A T I O N: On the Surface, around
and in the Lombok Strait
Owen Pasquerly
Crack Shot

Owen perched on the edge of his bunk, yawning and scratching his head. He was nearly knocked down as Eddie pushed his way through the crowded aisle in the forward torpedo room before plunking down on a middle bunk. Billy Fedder groggily tried to shove Haverly away, before sighing and rolling to the edge of his narrow cot.

"Ah, why don't you let poor Fedder sleep and go someplace else?" grumbled Nick, who lay in his bunk drawing a diagram of the boat's vent systems.

"Because I want to be where all you guys can see me. And Fedder can listen up or lose out," replied Eddie. "I got big news this time. Captain unsealed his orders. We're going—"

"Attention. All hands." The captain's voice came out of the little speaker in the forward torpedo room. Eddie's face turned glum.

"We're about to enter the heart of the War Zone. We'll hook up with our partner sub, the *Oarfish*, to form a wolfpack. Our mission is to sink as many Japanese ships as we can. We got assigned a hot spot: the South China Sea—"

Enrique started to beat on his chest. Owen gave out a whoop and hollered, "We'll sure see some action there!"

The captain continued: "But the Japanese won't be keen on letting us get there. They'll have some mines waiting to blow us up in the Lombok Strait. It'll take some fancy maneuvering, but we'll make it. Captain out."

"I wanted to tell," said Eddie. But the others paid no attention to him. The whoops and cheers had stopped. They sat in silence, the only sounds being the whispers of air in the ventilation tubes and the churning of the diesel engines.

Finally, Tom slowly said: "I sure hope the skipper knows what he's doing. Lombok Strait's a real bottleneck."

"Geez. We could get it right there—*glub, glub, glub,* down we go, and before we even get into the action," added Enrique.

Owen gave a low whistle.

"It's not Navy to whistle," snapped Eric. He'd been on a war patrol before and knew these things. "Shut up, you guys. Hey—he could have taken us through the Bali Strait, and then what? Raff Abbott's a famous skipper, don't you dumbbutts know that? He's not going to get us blown up."

Mr. Anderson ducked through the little door separating the forward torpedo room from the officer's quarters. "Pasquerly in here?" he asked, glancing around the compartment.

"Here, sir," said Owen, twisting himself up from under his torpedo.

"Pasquerly, skipper said you're to report for gunnery detail. There may be some floating mines before we approach Lombok. Skipper wants you back below before we actually get there, but—something about 'keeping you in mind'—anyway, he wants you to get to the gun locker now."

Gingersnaps. He remembered. "Yes, sir!" Owen replied,

FLOATING MINES

A mine is a hidden bomb that will go off if something bigger than a wave or a porpoise bumps against it. It is about three feet in diameter, studded with horns. Mines were attached to cords, or cables, from the ocean floor, awaiting a submarine. Sometimes one floated loose. It could be ignited if one of the horns was hit by a gun, and sunk if the shell was punctured.

tumbling out of his bunk and tripping over the sleeping Billy Fedder. Ace Evans and Buzz Gretz were breaking open the gun locker when Owen arrived. Ace was an OK guy, but Buzz was always nasty. They stared at him. Owen could tell they both were wondering, *Why'd the Old Man choose him?* But for once, Buzz didn't rag him. Owen knew he wouldn't dare, because this came straight from the captain.

A dry, metallic smell came out of the locker when they pulled the hatch open. It was full of Tommy guns, a couple of .45 pistols, some twelve-gauge double-barreled shotguns, Browning automatic rifles, and, at the back of the locker, Owen spied a .22 caliber rifle.

"What's your pleasure, Pasquerly? You get your pick," said Ace.

"I'll take the .22," replied Owen.

"That thing? We just keep it here for Mr. Zelks. Says he wants it to hunt dingoes when we go on leave in Australia."

"It's like my gun at home."

"Well, we're going to shoot stray mines. It's not a combat situation, so you can choose a peashooter far as I'm concerned, but that thing's single shot, you know."

"I know it is."

"So, Mountain Boy. You shoot skunk and squirrels for dinner back where you came from?" asked Buzz.

"I shoot 'em," replied Owen, ignoring Buzz's sarcasm about dinner.

He turned the rifle over in his hands, then bounced it across his arms, to get the feel of it.

Ace laughed. "Kind of like that thing, huh?"

"It's OK," replied Owen shrugging his shoulders, hiding his excitement.

They went up to the bridge to take their positions. It was nearly dusk when Owen spied something on the waves. For a moment he thought it was a sea turtle. The lolling, brown thing bobbed up and down, but it stayed in place. Not like a turtle. It was a mine, and Owen knew it was chock full of explosives. He heard Buzz and Ace cock their triggers. They fired. They missed.

Owen raised his gun to his shoulder. When he shot at an elk or a rabbit, he could sense what the animal would do. That's how he knew exactly when to squeeze the trigger. But he had solid ground under him then. Now, he had a target that bounced up and down, and he was bouncing, too, with the swell and dip of the *Mako*.

Owen felt a tension through his body. His legs measured the rhythm of the waves under him, while his arms and shoulders calculated the bounce of the target and—somehow—the rest of him knew how to bring these movements into sync. He squeezed the trigger. *KABOOOM!* The mine exploded. Water shot straight up in the air like a geyser.

He heard laughter behind him. It was Captain Abbott and, next to him, Mr. Anderson. "Great shooting, Pasquerly!" exclaimed the skipper. "How come we didn't discover you before for gunnery?"

Owen flushed and grinned, catching out of the corner of his eye the looks of begrudging respect from Buzz and Ace. "Thanks, Cap'n," he murmured.

There was one other mine they shot at before darkness fell and they were ordered below. Owen missed that time. The others got it. But he'd made the first, perfect shot—and that was enough.

Owen baked his bread, as usual, that night. Made doughnuts, too. Even a pot of soup—Smitty had shown him how—for feeding the 12to4s and the officers. They were all up that night, carefully navigating the Lombok Strait. When they got tired, they came to Owen for something good to eat.

Owen kept playing it back in his head while shaping and patting his bread dough—the captain's laugh and the admiring looks of the gunnery crew. Pop never looked at him like that. Right now, Pop seemed worlds away, and unimportant. He didn't feel angry with Pop: he just felt part of something better.

Now and then, Owen could feel the sub shift a few degrees left or right, beyond the normal light roll and swell of the boat. These weren't big enough to make his measuring cups fly off the counter if the boat lurched and he'd forgotten to hang them up. *I got that mine in one shot. One shot. The captain and the guys saw.* Now, he was keeping them fed. A baker—and a crack shot.

He was content. But then again, he didn't have to think about what was happening topside, as the *Mako* snaked her way through the Lombok Strait.

LOCATION: U.S.S. Mako's Patrol
Quadrant, South China Sea: Nighttime
Raff Abbott
"Battle Stations"

Raff propped his lanky frame against the bulkhead, enjoying the slight vibration seeping into his back from the *Mako's* engines. He'd just stepped out of the radio shack and was puzzling over how strange it was that neither the *Oarfish* nor the *Mako* had encountered any Empire ships so far on this patrol. Since clearing the Lombok Strait, the check-in communiqué with his wolfpack partner the last nine nights had read: "No enemy sightings. Holding course."

The crew was getting bored and restless for some action. *Ah, well,* Raff thought. *It'll come soon. This war isn't over yet. Nowhere close to over.* He stretched as he inhaled the clean night air flowing down the hatch of the surfaced sub. *Time to turn in—just need to stop off for a snack and write directives in my Night Orders book.* It was an hour past midnight.

Raff was composing in his mind a routine message about the currents ahead, speed to maintain, and the conditions under which he should be awakened. He lost his train of thought as he entered the crew's mess.

A group of 12to4s on their break sat straddling the benches playing a card game. At the moment Raff entered, Enrique Romero tossed down his cards. Suddenly, he scratched his mop of glossy black hair. "Geez! When are we going to get to fight some Japs!?"

Raff saw Tom Benson and Eric Edison shifting their gaze from Romero over to him, with a "there's the captain" look in their eyes. Romero spun around, looking embarrassed.

Raff tried not to laugh. He had an image to maintain, after all. But Romero looked pretty strange shaking his red-goggled head like some alien lion.

"Well, Romero, I don't know when we'll sniff out an enemy ship, but maybe you can be our mascot and just scare them to death?"

"Hey, whatever it takes, Cap'n. But I'd sorta rather bring 'em down with a few torpedoes."

Raff liked Romero's ability to take a ribbing. And he knew he could count on Tom Benson to ask pointed questions, so he wasn't surprised to hear:

"All kidding aside, Captain—when do you think it will be?"

"It's a big ocean, Benson. The South China Sea is a million square miles. Even our quadrant of it is huge. Could be we'll—" but Charlie Zelks's voice on the intercom interrupted the conversation.

"Captain Abbott to the bridge! Smoke plume off the starboard bow!"

The special cards for the red-blind lookouts flew in all directions as the 12to4s tripped over the benches and scrambled to their feet. Raff sprinted into the control room and up the ladder to the conning tower, then up the conning tower ladder through the hatch to the bridge.

"What've you got?"

"Unidentified vessel. Presumed enemy. Gallagher spotted it, sir."

"I'm still night blind. Was planning to go to bed instead of dashing up here. Can you see it yet, Charlie?"

"Through the binocs. I'm getting a black flutter. That moon's like a spotlight on it. It's still very wispy, though."

"You sure you remember a smoke plume from a whale blow, right?"

"Somewhere dim in my brain—yeah, I think I can sort that out, Captain."

There was still time for some kidding before a battle heated up. Raff knew this was the beginning of a long wait of tracking that smoke plume, seeing the ship but avoiding being seen, and plotting strategy for a successful attack. They needed to conserve their energy, and he knew Charlie knew it as well as he did. He wanted the others to sense that they were relaxed and pacing themselves.

"I'm putting the tracking party on it," said Raff, as he swiveled himself into the hatch and down the ladder to the conning tower. Expectant faces turned toward him, knowing it was the captain who called the shots—literally. The captain planned when to pursue a vessel, when to fire torpedoes, how deep to set the torpedoes, when to surface, when to dive— and when to get the heck away. Paul Anderson, his youngest officer, looked blank and tense. Raff knew it would be Paul's first battle.

He winked at Paul. This was serious business. But it worked best if you played it like it was a game. And Raff was a good hunter.

WOLFPACKS

"Wolfpacks" of two or more submarines were common in the Pacific in World War II. "Ben's Busters," "Hydeman's Hellcats," and "Clarey's Crushers" were some of them, named for the senior skipper. They made loosely coordinated attacks with one sub striking and the other completing the sinkings. Typically, there was a designated daily rendezvous time to exchange messages and orders. Communication could be on the surface by radar, megaphone, or blinker or by coded messages on a special radio frequency. Codes and signals were routinely used. For example, "Dog Dog Seagull" means a submarine had to dive to avoid a plane.

TORPEDO DATA COMPUTER (TDC)

Computers as we know them today, with memory "chips," did not exist in WWII. The TDC was a mechanical analog computer with a complex series of interconnecting dials and cranks. Located on the bulkhead (wall) next to the periscope, the TDC made it possible for the captain to shift targets and change attack plans quickly, and still have a good likelihood of making a hit. Each time the captain tracked the movement of the target, data on its route, how fast it was going and how far away it was from the submarine were entered into the TDC. The TDC then calculated settings for the torpedoes as they were fired. Besides the periscope, it was the most important piece of attack equipment on the boat.

"I think we've just made our first contact. Let's show the *Oarfish* how it's done," said Raff with a grin, as he clicked on the intercom: "Tracking party to the conning tower!"

In seconds, the tracking party crowded into the conning tower. One by one, their heads emerged from the hole cut in the deck as they pulled themselves up the ladder and spun into the tower, their sandals banging on the sheet metal deck. Raff thought again how the conning tower reminded him of a tree house.

He gave his officers their orders.

"Gallagher spotted a plume, so it's time to track it. No sleep for anybody tonight. Paul—you're on plot. Watch that ship—or it could be a small convoy. See if it zigzags. Plot their movements on a graph. Look for a pattern."

Raff turned to Charlie, his right-hand man.

"Charlie, you've got the TDC. I'd like to stay on the surface for a while to end-run the target—get ahead of it, then submerge and wait to fire."

"Aye, Cap'n!" He hitched up his pants like he was about to mount a horse.

Raff clicked on the intercom to the maneuvering room. "Itty, stand by to put all four engines on line." Chief Itty's gravelly voice crackled back through the intercom:

"Aye, Cap'n. Got it."

"Paul, it's your honor to sound the first battle stations alarm of this war patrol. Go to it!"

"Aye, sir!" Paul flushed and nodded at Raff, then dropped down the ladder to the control room, his feet not even touching the rungs.

Ding! Ding! Ding! "All hands. Man your battle stations. Battle stations." Sailors walked fast, hearts pounding, but in orderly precision, to their posts: posts they knew well from practice—but this wasn't practice.

Then came the quiet as everyone settled into their positions. They were hunters now, stalking, calculating. There was no goofing around: the crew focused and moved as one organism.

"Definitely two ships," came the report from the radar station, breaking the silence. "Big one, with an escort weaving around it."

Paul called up from the control room. "They're zigzagging, Skipper, but it's a regular pattern. True course zero-nine-zero, due east."

Raff, amazed, drew in his breath and leaned a hand on the periscope. "Look's like a beam shot! He's giftwrapping himself for us. That escort's going to be hopping mad, because we're going to get what he's guarding." He flipped on the intercom to the maneuvering room. "Itty, rev 'em up."

"Aye, Cap'n!"

"Helm! Right full rudder!"

"Aye, Cap'n! Right full rudder!"

Clicks and whirs sounded as Charlie twirled in position information and the TDC's dials spun out the calculations to guide the torpedoes on their deadly course. The two engines that had been powering the sub were joined by the other two, growling and churning, surging the *Mako* forward, then hard right, to starboard, as she began her race to outdistance the Japanese vessels. But those vessels had not detected the American sub, and, under Raff's skillful handling, they would not have a clue they were being pursued: would have no warning before torpedoes blew one of them apart.

BEAM SHOT

A beam shot is the ideal setup for firing torpedoes. The target's side, its entire length, is exposed to the submarine, greatly increasing the chances the sub will sink it.

"Cap'n, we're just ahead of them. We can see two plumes now."

"Good. Lookouts below. Clear the bridge. Sound the diving alarm. We're going to close in. Dive! Dive!"

AhOOOOgah! AhOOOOOOgah!

Nick, Enrique, and Eddie vaulted down the ladder to the conning tower and swung themselves over and down the next ladder to the control room. A spray of salt water had already washed across the bridge and cascaded into the conning tower and onto their heads before the hatch above them was sealed.

Raff turned to his helmsman. "Helm, come right forty-five degrees." Then leaning over the open hole to the control room, Raff hollered:

"Paul, trim out at sixty-five feet," thinking for a split second about how good Paul had become at diving since the embarrassment of his first dive.

The *Mako's* bow pointed downward, and Raff, almost by instinct, adjusted his stance, tilting from his belly to keep upright. He heard the crush of pounding ocean waves over his head, pelting against the bridge and engulfing the *Mako*. Then, when the proper exchange of water between tanks had been achieved, the *Mako* leveled at sixty-five feet below the ocean's surface—and crept in for the attack.

L O C A T I O N: Patrol Quadrant of the
U.S.S. Mako, South China Sea: Nighttime
Raff Abbott
Piece of Cake

There was silence under the surface of the ocean, except for the hiss and whoosh of air from the *Mako*'s vents and, in the forward torpedo room, the muffled clunk-grind of the bow planes turning up and, in the after torpedo room, the thrumbing of the propeller screws. Navigation and calculation told Raff the *Mako* was almost directly in front of two enemy vessels. But he needed to look up through the periscope to confirm that. A dangerous look, if the Japanese spotted the slim metal rod emerging from the waves.

"Ready to take a peek, Captain?" asked Charlie Zelks, turning from the TDC. The two men exchanged a glance that spoke of danger. And sport.

"Sure. Now's a fine time for a peek—fifteen seconds." Raff crouched, extending his arms to grab the periscope as it ascended from its well. He wouldn't expose it long; his eyes had been trained to see very quickly. "Up scope!"

Raff swiveled the periscope 360 degrees and saw what he hoped to. A big ship—unarmed, probably an oil tanker. But it wasn't alone. There was a protector ship, an escort. He recognized

"BEARING—MARK!"

The captain must figure out the target's size, speed, position, and where they are heading in order to calculate how to aim the torpedoes. He takes a series of observations through the periscope that are fed into the torpedo data computer to help him establish a firing setup.

it at once as a *chidori:* a lethal little antisubmarine ship. Raff zeroed in on the big one: "Tipped funnel forward, twin small stacks aft, low riding. Angle on the bow seventy-five degrees starboard. Bearing—mark! Down scope!" slapping the handles as the chrome tube swiveled back down. "Beautiful setup!"

Charlie had read "310" as the degree mark from the outer rim of the periscope position as Raff called "bearing—mark!" and dialed it into the TDC. Paul flipped through the manual of known Japanese ships, for an identification of the target.

"It's a *maru,* a tanker, Cap'n!"

"Good. Make ready all bow tubes. Open outer doors. I want the electric fish set to launch." Raff held up his thumb to signal "up scope" for another check. No change in the target, but that could still happen—in a matter of seconds their setup could be worthless. "Down scope! Set torpedoes for eight feet depth. Range: fifteen hundred yards."

"Looks good. Fire when ready," said Charlie, as the TDC whirled and spun its orders to set the torpedoes. "Up scope!" ordered Raff once more to be sure they were in position to hit the oiler, not the escort. They wouldn't have time to get both. Raff was satisfied.

"Fire one!"

"One fired!" Raff waited ten seconds for the torpedo to clear the sub.

"Fire two!

"Two fired!" Another ten seconds.

"Fire three!"

"Three fired!"

The *Mako* recoiled from the jolt of the departing torpedoes.

"All three running hot, straight, and normal," reported Tom Benson, who could interpret the slightest changes in underwater sounds. Hot, straight, and normal. Just the words Raff wanted to hear.

At 114 seconds, by a stopwatch, there was a *KrrrrrrVhoooom!* Then, ten seconds later, *VHOOOM!* Two hits!

The *Mako* shuddered and swayed, engulfed by roiling water.

"Up scope!" yelled Raff. Through his bobbing eyepiece he witnessed a hellish scene of flames soaring into the night sky, then springing like some mad imp back and forth across the tanker's deck. The big stack crumpled, sheet metal twisted like tin foil—then ship, flames, and seawater braided together in a gigantic explosion. The enraged *chidori*, lit up to red orange in the ghastly glow, turned hard about to pursue the *Mako*.

"Take her deep! Pull us to port, then rig for silent running! Escort's on us!"

In under a minute and a half, the *Mako* had descended to 300 feet below the surface. Ventilation and motors were cut. Sounds carry in water; the *chidori* would be listening, beyond the terrible ripping sounds of metal bulkheads and the booms of exploding oil from the wounded ship. Listening, to pick up by her sonar, any clue as to where the submarine had gone. Now it would be a hide-and-seek game: but this time the *Mako* was on the defensive.

Tom, looking intent as he strained to hear through the sonar earphones, announced in a low voice: "Debris floating down, but it's coming slow, and off to starboard. Doesn't sound like it will hit us."

Raff nodded. They may have been able to pull out far enough. "Pings?"

Tom shook his head, but Raff saw his lips moving wordlessly, as if he was hearing something else—and trying to sort out

UNDERWATER NOISE AND PURSUIT

The pursuing ship uses sound wave patterns ("pings") from sonar to try to locate a submerged submarine. Normally, pings can be heard throughout the boat. The submarine has its own sonar, to hear ocean noises and interpret which are dangerous. The two dreaded sounds are these "pings" and the click . . . blaam! of oil drums ("ash cans") exploding. This is called depth charging, because the charges are set to explode in the ocean's depths to blow up—and sink—a submarine.

what it meant. But in an instant he knew. They all knew. The *chidori* was flinging "ash cans" down on them.

The breaking-up sounds of the doomed oiler had ceased. Muffled sounds like fireworks exploding in the distance surrounded the *Mako*. But only a few. And far away. The escort hadn't been able to pinpoint the submarine's location for good aim of its depth charges.

Tom's voice was low again, but the tension had left it. "Captain, I hear his screws. He's not circling—he's heading away from us!"

Raff nodded and replied, "He's turning to pick up survivors from the oiler. Tell me when all noise from the screws has stopped." A long moment elapsed.

"We're clear, Captain!"

Raff sounded the order throughout the boat: "Secure from silent running. Continue on course."

Raff stood still a moment, letting in the realization that he was the pivot point of all this action and destruction. His instincts and training had saved his boat, and destroyed another. Lives were lost. The enemy—but lives. Now thousands of gallons of oil would never reach Japan. It wouldn't cripple their war effort, but it would make a dent in it. And that he felt good about.

Below the conning tower, floating up from the control room, Raff heard the whoops and boasts of the crew. He recognized the voices of Owen Pasquerly and Enrique Romero guffawing about "what was the big thing about depth charging?" and "piece of cake!"

Piece of cake is right, thought Raff, rubbing his bleary, sleep-deprived eyes. *This was too easy.* Next time would likely be a far fiercer battle for the fighting shark submarine.

L O C A T I O N: Shallow Waters of the
South China Sea: On the Surface
Nick Gallagher
Flying Fish and Achilles' Heel

Nick clomped and dripped into the crew's mess. Flying fish wriggled in his rain poncho as he held them against his stomach. They'd flung themselves onto the deck; Nick gathered them up, figuring they'd make a good meal.

Owen was finishing his bread baking for the night. Smitty laid out eggs and canned tomatoes for breakfast. Enrique swayed between the cooling bread and the waiting eggs, doing a slow dance. The radio played a song popular back home: "I got a gal in Kal—a—ma—ZOO—ZOO—ZOO!"

Nick was about to tell Enrique to stop his goofy dancing and help clean the fish when the song stopped. They were too far out to sea to get any radio shows except what the Japanese broadcast, just to make them nuts. The sultry voice of Tokyo Rose floated above him, from the radio mounted on the bulkhead.

"Did you like that song, boys?" she purred. "I do have the best show in the Pacific, don't you think? I chose this one because I'll bet some of you have girls back home. Do you miss them? It's really too bad your loved ones will be losing you forever . . . "

Enrique flipped his nose up at the radio. "Yeah, Rosie? Sez you!" He laughed. Owen giggled. Smitty grunted.

"It's most unfortunate you face certain death at the hands of the Japanese Empire." Nick made himself laugh, but the cruel words said in that catlike voice were creepy.

"So, you ain't told us what yer doing carryin' around those fish," said Smitty. "You hintin' at me for something? How about you get some more and clean 'em, and I'll serve 'em up with first shift's breakfast."

"That'd be great, Smitty," said Nick. Then he smiled sneakily at Enrique. "You and Owen clean them. You get the fish guts. I'll keep bringing them down."

"Fish cleaning. Pee-ee-euw," Enrique wrinkled his nose at the flopping fish Nick had dumped on a mess bench.

Nick quickly tucked his rain poncho under his arm to go back on the bridge before Enrique could argue. His watch had ended at 4 a.m., but when he was able to get permission, he liked to come back up to see the dawn. The sun lifting up, shooting out gold rays and the waves shifting from black to blue was something worth looking at. Nick wasn't real religious, but it always felt to him like a blessing—a reminder of something grand out there that was easy to forgot about.

"Permission to come topside, sir?"

"Granted. Come back up, Gallagher," said Mr. Zelks. "We've got flying fish all over the place. But we'll be submerging soon, with the daylight, so hurry up."

Mr. Zelks was folding up his sextant after taking star readings. One of these days Nick hoped to get a demonstration of how pointing a little gizmo at stars could show where on the globe the submarine was. But right now there were fish to gather. So many that Nick had to watch his head as the flyers arched over the waves and onto the *Mako's* deck.

"Why do they do that, Mr. Zelks? Fly up, I mean," he asked, sucking his bleeding finger, cut from the splayed fin of a flier.

"Escaping predators, I'd guess. I saw a shark fin weaving around here a few minutes ago."

Nick ducked as another fish came toward his head. It sprayed saltwater droplets into his hair, then smacked as it hit his outspread poncho. But its fins fanned out, and, with a spasm, it bounced free. He was running out of time, so he pulled two fish, slippery and fresh smelling, from between the periscope shears, and went back below as the sub dived.

"There's sure a lot of sea life around here," Nick said as he plunked down by Enrique and Owen. Nick could see Owen knew how to clean a fish. Enrique scowled, his arms coated in scales and fish guts. A "hrrumph" sound came from Smitty as he prepared breakfast on the galley stove.

Nick looked at Enrique and Owen. They both shrugged.

"How are you doing in there, Smitty?" asked Nick. He'd learned by now that grunts and mumbles from Smitty meant he wanted someone to pay attention to him.

"Lotta sea life, you say! That's not the only thing you oughta be noticin' around here."

"What else, Smitty?" asked Owen, his filet knife deftly cutting under a fin.

"Shallow. Too dang shallow in these parts of the South China. Water's too clear. Pretty, oh, sure. But we can't dive deep. Don't like this shallow stuff. No sir."

"You suppose the skipper's thought about that?" asked Owen. Nick gave him a warning glance, but it was too late.

Somehow Owen must have forgotten how loyal Smitty was to the captain: they'd served together on the *Oarfish*.

Owen shrank back when Smitty banged his iron skillet down on the stovetop. Nick was surprised at how Owen looked. Back home, he could always tell at the farm auctions if an animal had been mistreated. It was jumpy. Just like Owen was right now.

"*Thought* about it! *Thought* about it! This ain't some greenie skipper. This here's Rafferty Abbott. He's got some reason for pokin' around here. He knows some scuttlebutt we ain't heard about. Mark my words!"

"Yeah, Smitty. Must be," said Nick. He wanted to cheer Owen up, and he felt edgy himself, so was about to tell a joke when he glanced back at Enrique.

A devilish spark lit Enrique's eyes as he lunged at Nick's ear. Enrique was always teasing Nick for his big ears that stood out from his head. Nick felt fish slime in his ear. But he grabbed a wad of yellow gut and lunged back at Enrique, streaking the mustache Enrique was so proud of. Owen whooped and tossed a fin like it was a boomerang, winging both Nick and Enrique. A glare from Smitty sobered them up.

"Fish guts ain't a smell I want to be sniffin' the rest of this war patrol."

Nick got up to fetch a water bucket and rags.

"What's the movie today?" asked Owen, changing the subject. "Not that Christmas one again, I hope."

"Not Christmas. That Spencer Tracy one, where he's a zoomie who crashes his plane and goes to heaven and has to watch some other guy get sweet with his girl. I've seen it six times," moaned Enrique, wringing out the dishrag and emptying it in the bucket.

"Don't worry, Romeo," said Nick. "That won't happen to you. What girl would want anybody else after knowing you?"

Enrique swelled up his chest. "Yup."

That night, instead of a radio check-in with the *Oarfish*, the two boats met on the open sea. It was a calm night, so they were able to come side to side. Captain Jones paddled a raft over to the *Mako* and shimmied up a rope to the bridge. Nick saw in amazement that with him was Lieutenant Baine, his old teacher from sub school!

"Well, as I live and breathe! It's Nick Gallagher!" Lieutenant Baine stood with his hands on his hips, shouting up at Nick on his lookout perch. A duffle bag was slung over his shoulder. "Brought a movie to trade. A western. Good one, too." Nick heard the metal reels of film clank in the bag.

"How ya doing, Lieutenant?" asked Nick. "Do you like the *Oarfish?*"

"Doin' great. The *Oarfish*'s a fine boat. But you know better than to talk on lookout duty. I'm going below. Catch you later."

It felt funny to see his old teacher out here. Sub school was so far away.

Nick looked at the two skippers, Captain Abbott and Captain Jones. Their faces were shadowed as they talked. With the noise of the engines and batteries charging up, he could only make out a few words: "convoy," "fifty feet," and something that sounded like "magic," which didn't make sense.

After the visitors returned to the *Oarfish*, the subs continued to cruise together. Their bows sliced through the lapping moonlit waves of the South China Sea.

MAGIC: THE SECRET TO DIE FOR

It is said that a big secret can't be kept. But, throughout most of World War II, a group of top officials knew the primary communications code of the Japanese—a code the Japanese felt could never be broken. This meant that intercepted messages from the Japanese could be deciphered. Whenever a radioman picked up something coded "MAGIC" (or ULTRA), that message could be given only to the captain to decode. This is how it was known that Admiral Isoroku Yamamoto, the brilliant commander of the Japanese Navy, would be traveling on a certain airplane at a certain time. That plane was destroyed. Another life lost because of MAGIC was that of Captain John Cromwell, on the U.S.S. *Sculpin*. Rather than be captured by the Japanese and possibly forced to reveal his knowledge of MAGIC, he elected to go down with the submarine when it was fatally depth-charged. The other men on the submarine drowned or were taken as POWs (prisoners of war) by the Japanese.

Nick was back up on the bridge after his break when he heard a shout from the conning tower: "Something on the radar, range twenty-five thousand yards, bearing one three one true. I've got a dot cluster. Probably a tropical storm."

Captain Abbott hadn't gone to bed like he usually did this time of night. He was still on the bridge. "Let me have a look." The skipper dropped down the hatch into the conning tower, only to reappear a few moments later.

"Storm, my aunt Sally! That's no storm. That's a whole Japanese convoy! Stop the battery charge."

A whoop jumped up Nick's throat before he even felt it coming. All the fellows were whooping and stomping. The skipper cupped his hands and shouted over to Captain Jones on the *Oarfish*. "Hey, Jake! We've got 'em on radar. Has to be the convoy we've been looking for!"

"We just picked them up, too! Let's gear up and go blast 'em!"

"Jake, you go five miles north. *Mako* will attack first, from the south, forcing the ones we don't get up your way."

"Well—be sure you leave some for us!" came the *Oarfish* reply for everyone on deck to hear. The captain turned to Nick. "You'll be right in the middle of the action, Gallagher. We're going to need those eyes of yours."

Nick could barely concentrate on keeping his binoculars up to look for smoke plumes on the horizon. The captain had chosen him. He'd get to be topside. He'd *have* to be topside. This wasn't just one ship with an escort, like the tanker. It was a whole convoy! Could be there were a bunch of supply ships and tankers. Could be even cruisers and battleships and destroyers. He'd always heard a submarine shouldn't try to take on a destroyer. Two submarines against—how many ships? It was then that another feeling tingled in him, like an electric wire. He was scared.

When Nick went below, the hubbub had died down. The air was dense with a concentration he could almost feel, like rubbing his hand on a thick towel. He saw Mr. Anderson and Mr. Zelks in the control room, poring over sea charts and staring at the fathometer. Worry was etched on their faces. Nick didn't know a lot about the charts they were looking at, except that they showed, like the fathometer, the depth of the waters below them and ahead. Smitty's grumblings rumbled back into his head: "Don't like this shallow stuff. No sir."

Lieutenant Baine had told them in sub school: "A submarine has an Achilles' heel. It can't dive to escape from enemy bombing when there isn't enough water to dive into."

Was Tokyo Rose right? Her voice purred again in Nick's brain: "You face death at the hands of the Japanese Empire."

Shallow water.

A whole convoy.

Him topside in the battle.

L O C A T I O N: Shallows of the South
China Sea
Raff Abbott
Enrique Romero
Convoy

Running his hand through his straw-colored hair, Raff gave a rueful grin. He sat with his officers, crowding around the linoleum table in the wardroom. "This is the big one," he said. "I guess we all know that. Risky. But that's why we're here."

He watched Paul, with his elbows on his knees, slowly rubbing his hands together. Charlie tugged at a coil of his curly hair. They could feel the sweat and tickle of hair on each other's legs: the jump of one another's muscles from the excitement and tension of the coming battle. Raff felt like they were all wearing the same skin.

"How many ships are there? I mean—how outnumbered are we?" asked Paul.

"How outnumbered? Any one of those ships outnumbers us if they see us before we can attack," said Raff. "They're bigger than we are. We just have to be sure they don't see us."

Turning to Charlie, Raff asked, "You think they've got radar?"

Charlie folded his arms and sucked in his breath. "I'm betting they have it, especially if the convoy has battleships. Not like the *chidori* and tanker we nailed last time. We've been keeping out of radar range. But the closer we get, the likelier it is they'll pick us up. Of course, it's night, and there's a cloud cover over the stars, so that's on our side."

Raff nodded. "What's up ahead?"

Charlie unrolled a chart and smoothed it flat on the table. Full of shaded lines and numbers, it was a grid showing the ocean's topography.

"It's not the surface I'm worried about: it's what's under us. We're in shallow water—thirty fathoms—a hundred and eighty feet. If we engaged in battle right here, we couldn't do a deep dive to evade depth charging. The chart and the fathometer are both telling us that."

"Right. But I'm betting it will be deeper at our intercept point," said Raff.

"I like the sound of that," Charlie replied. "The further east we can be when we attack, the better."

"Charlie, you'll be in the conning tower. Paul, you'll be in the forward torpedo room. I'll be topside, on the bridge, with Gallagher to help me see the targets."

"Captain," said Paul, "Gallagher's not battle-tested. I wonder if he's the right choice to be topside."

"He's got the best night vision of anyone on the *Mako*," said Raff. "That makes him the best choice, even if it'll be—" He paused. "—not a whole lot of fun."

Raff raised his hand as if to thump on the table. It was his habit to signal that a conference was over. But he let his hand drop back onto his lap.

"We're probably in for a rough ride. And a long night. I'm glad—and proud—to have you with me. Just wanted to say that. So let's get 'em."

Then Raff slapped his hand on the table.

"They've lit warning flares! The Japs' radar must've picked us up!"

Mr. Zelks's voice crackled over the intercom throughout the *Mako*. Enrique felt as if a warning flare had gone off inside his stomach instead of out over the water. The battle had begun, and the intercom was his only way to know what was happening.

"Then let's make 'em dizzy! Give me a reverse spinner!" yelled the captain. "Helm, hard about! Bring us west, now give me north! OK! Give me east!"

The *Mako* deftly spun to confuse her prey: one way, then the opposite direction, twirling like the slim dial on a compass. Enrique and his buddies in the forward torpedo room grabbed on to chains, pipes, bunk rims, and torpedo mounts—anything to ride out the merry-go-round until the *Mako* stopped spinning.

"What's going on now?" wailed Eddie. There were fumbling and popping noises over the intercom. Enrique looked up at the little black speaker, in the snaky tangle of cords and pipes. Then it sputtered back to life.

"We're in the center of the convoy! There's a cargo vessel, a couple of tankers, and—what's that—two destroyers, a transport ship, and some unidentifieds. I count twelve ships!"

Twelve ships! And one submarine. Us, thought Enrique, exhilarated and terrified.

"Clear the bridge! Just Gallagher and me stay up," came the captain's voice through the scratchy speaker. *If only a submarine had windows. Even a peephole,* thought Enrique. He wanted to see his torpedoes blaze away and blow up the Jap ships in the night. But he was glad it was dark topside. The mottled gray *Mako* would be hard to see.

"Charlie! How's that fathometer?"

"Still shallow, but we're all right to dive if we keep going east!"

"Destroyer! It's . . . closing . . . in on us. Coming fast!" came Nick's voice, almost stuttering.

"Get a bearing on it," said the captain.

"They're too close! Can't . . . get a bearing!" yelled Nick.

"Hard right, or we'll ram 'em!" answered the captain.

Bazing! Bazzzziiiing! TataTat!

Muffled sounds of Japanese bullets whizzed by the *Mako*. Enrique couldn't stop himself from hunching down, dodging bullets he couldn't see.

"Charlie! Looks like the Fourth of July at midnight up here! Get me a firing setup pronto!" came the captain's voice through the speaker.

"Got it! Fire anytime."

"Then bow tubes: give 'em two."

"That's us!" yelled Enrique. "You're done for, you Japs." Enrique quivered and slapped at his thighs. *Where's the blast? Shouldn't be so long. Where is it?*

The torpedoes missed!

Mr. Zelks's voice came over the intercom: "Destroyer evaded, Cap'n. It moved behind that tanker. Setup's ready. Two thousand yards . . . fifteen hundred . . . eleven hundred . . ."

"Fire one! Tip to starboard rudder. Fire two—three—four!" ordered the captain.

Enrique pressed his firing key down. Air rushed into the tube, sucking and thunking as it hit the torpedo and shoved it out into the ocean. Enrique sniffed in the smell of burnt powder from the igniter, lighting the gases inside the torpedo. "Go blast 'em, baby!" he shouted. Eddie fired, then Enrique again and Tom. The *Mako* rocked and recoiled after each fish went out. Now the tubes in the forward room were empty.

KaBOOOMM!

"Got it!" Everyone whooped and hollered. Enrique yelled: "That was my fish!" The ripping, exploding ship made a tidal wave; the *Mako* bounced up over the surface and slapped down. Enrique's stomach lifted and slammed. He felt sick. *Got 'em. Got 'em.*

Loading torpedoes in the forward torpedo room

"Tanker split clear in half. Sunk in thirty seconds. And a hit on a cargo vessel—but he's not down, he's going to get us!" came a voice from the intercom that sounded like Nick. "The water's burning! Oil on the water. Watch out, Cap'n! Flames are jumping over here!"

"Forward's out of fish! We've got a setup on the after tubes!"

"Then let's show him our backside," growled the captain. "Half speed. Give him four fish."

The *Mako* spun around. She shuddered and shook again as more torpedoes sought the destroyer. Enrique counted seconds. Lost track. Began again. How could it take so long?

"It's a hit! Midsection exploded!"

Mr. Anderson hollered: "Reload! Reload! Put your back into it!"

Enrique hefted and squeezed and pushed with the others to lift a new torpedo off its rack. Chains clanked and the clamp made a deep *sproing* sound as it was unleashed. "Get that torpedo into tube number one! Hurry it up!"

Owen's elbow jabbed at Enrique's ribs. "Hey, watch it!" yelled Enrique. "This fish's heavier than all of us put together."

"Not my fault," squeaked Owen.

"Grab it!"

"Hang on!"

"Ah . . . oof!"

A metallic odor, powerful and sinister, mingled with the smells of diesel oil, sweat, and grime. Enrique shivered even though he was sweating. How could he carry this? But he had to carry it. Had to get even for Juan. Had to blow up more Japs.

Unnnhhh. Thunk. The torpedo was ready. The tube door wobbled and slammed.

"Fathometer at four hundred feet," said Mr. Zelks over the intercom. "Rigged for diving any time, Captain."

"Not yet." The captain gasped. "Give me more speed. Transport ship's coming for us. Gallagher sees him. He can't see us in the dark, but he knows more or less where we are."

"Can't squeeze out . . . speed, Cap'n!" Enrique caught fragments of what was being said as he crouched to help lift another torpedo. He felt strong enough now to lift a car, pumped up by the excitement of the attack. But sweat poured into his eyes and rolled off his arms and hands, making the torpedo hard to hold. *Hang on. Hang on. Lift.*

"We've got to fire now! Who's ready, forward or aft?" demanded the captain.

Mr. Anderson slapped at the intercom button. "Forward's got two in."

"Then fire one! Fire two!" Enrique's head buzzed. *How many seconds? Why can't I count right? Are they duds? C'mon, c'mon—hit!"*

KaBOOOOMMM!

The transport was hit.

Tatatat tat! The Japanese fired back at them, blindly, in the dark night trying to see through the smoke of explosions the ghostly gray submarine that spun on the surface like a mongoose darting with perfect balance to evade a cobra.

"Left full rudder. Let's slide away from that destroyer—"but the captain's voice was nearly drowned out by the sounds of the exploding transport. Enrique had never before today heard metal screech and wail. It was like an immense, living thing being torn in two.

"Sounds alive," he murmured, not even knowing he'd said it, until he heard Mr. Anderson say in a strange voice: "Better

View through the periscope of a sinking transport ship

we hear the ship scream than the men inside. That's a troop transport." But there was no more time to talk. More voices from the intercom sputtered and crackled overhead:

"After torpedo room's got two torps ready!"

"Then give me another spinner. I'm finishing off that cargo vessel," came the captain's voice.

The *Mako* spun again. Enrique grabbed at the chains hanging from the bulkhead. Maybe a shot would go through the bulkhead. Go right through him. Kill him. Today. *Ratatat bazziiing!* sounds echoed around him coming from ships he couldn't even see.

"You got the setup?" asked the captain impatiently.

Enrique couldn't see anything, but he imagined the *Mako*'s tail pointed at the cargo vessel, poised like a scorpion preparing to sting.

"Got it! Range, eight hundred yards!"

"Then half speed, and fire!"

KABOOOM! After the blast, there was a low rumble. Enrique could tell when the cargo ship had slid under when he felt waves pelt the *Mako*'s hull, then pull back. There was a sucking noise, like water going down a gigantic bathtub.

"Destroyer dead ahead! Zero angle on the bow! He's got a bone in his teeth!" Enrique recognized Nick's voice.

"Dive! Dive! Rig for silent running!" came the captain's voice. There were bumping and muffled noises on the intercom. Then the *Mako*'s nose dipped into her dive.

The bullet sounds blurred above Enrique's head. They'd hide now. They were diving to safety. *Everything's fine. Everything's fine—*

"Spike on the fathometer! We're going to—"

In the next instant, a thud and a scraping sound from the after section sent a teeth-jarring vibration throughout the submarine.

The *Mako* had been wounded. There was something besides sand below them.

"ZERO ANGLE ON THE BOW! BONE IN HIS TEETH!"

A ship is dead ahead, pointing straight at the bow of its enemy, when there is a "zero angle." It knows exactly where its opponent is and is likely getting ready to fight, in fury, to the death. If it charges at high speed to ram the other ship, waves will churn up in a frothing, curling pattern to either side of its bow, like a growling dog clenching a bone in its teeth. Many submarines, much smaller than the ship bearing down on them, faced this terrifying view from their bridge or through the periscope.

```
L O C A T I O N:   Under the South China Sea
Owen Pasquerly
Depth-Charged
```

Owen slipped off his sweaty leather sandals to run quick as a cat from the forward torpedo room to the galley. He didn't like hearing his friends asking, "What'd we hit?" and "Did it bust us open?" Anyway, Smitty might need help securing the mess and galley for silent running.

Owen kept himself upright during the steep dive, using the palms of his hands to bounce off the narrow corridor walls. He jostled and ducked under sailors, everyone running to get to their post before the doors between compartments were sealed. He felt the slap of his feet on the tile floor, but the familiar, safe sounds of the submerged sub weren't there: no *grind-thwap* of the bow planes, no whirring fans.

Smitty was spinning the bolt on the watertight door between the galley and the control room when Owen came up, panting, behind him. Owen felt safer with Smitty than being back in the torpedo room. Smitty was always rock-solid calm. But at the instant that Smitty turned around, they heard a clicking sound like a rifle cocking, then a *BAAMMM!* that nearly rocked them off their feet. Instinctively, Owen and Smitty looked up

SILENT RUNNING

Sound carries well underwater; sonar echo
ranging helps locate a submerged submarine—
which can't be seen from the surface—by the
returned sound patterns. Anything that makes
noise or consumes power that is not essential
for life preservation is shut down in silent
running: one of the most important defensive
tactics of the submarine. Lights are dimmed,
air conditioning and fans switched off, and
steering done by hand instead of hydraulically.
Watertight doors are sealed between
compartments to help prevent flooding the
entire boat if one area is hit, although a sub is
usually doomed anyway if this happens. The
attacker on the surface may wait many hours
in hopes of hearing a motor, the shout of a
panicked man, the clank of a dropped tool,
or the sound of a pump, to hone in on their
location for a well-placed depth charge—and
the kill.

toward what they couldn't see: a ship dropping bombs aimed at the *Mako*. Smitty's face turned white and his jaw tensed. "I won't never get used to them depth charges. They'll give us a good poundin' this time," he muttered.

Click . . . BAAAMM! Click . . . BAAAMM! Click . . . BAAAMM!

One after another the ash cans exploded around the *Mako*. If even one hit, that would be the end of the sub and all her hands.

Owen half-crawled over to a bench in the mess. Only then did he see Nick at a table in the corner. Nick's hair was sopping wet, his eyes were bloodshot, and he smelled burnt and smoky. He seemed to be in a trance.

"Hey, Nick! Your arms! And your shirt—what happened?"

Nick stared down at his bruise-covered arms as if they belonged to somebody else. Then, slowly, he pulled his shirt out. A look of surprise spread across his face, seeing the rips and singe marks.

Smitty said in a low voice: "Gallagher was topside in the battle. He and the cap'n both look like that. I seen 'em come down to the control room 'fore the dive. Let him be. He'll talk when he's ready."

Owen nodded, then whispered to Smitty: "We hit something during the dive. What was that?"

Smitty sighed and—to Owen's amazement—chuckled. "Now if *that* don't beat all. We got a skipper can maneuver and twirl in battle like one of them whirling dervishes. Then on the way down, he bonks into a sunk ship!"

"A ship? On the bottom?" asked Owen breathlessly.

"Yup. Freak accident. One in a thousand chance we'd bend our backside on a big 'un that sank pointin' up."

"Did we get hurt bad?"

"Well, if it was real bad, we'd be leakin' like crazy. Or worse. 'Fore I shut the door to the control room, I heard Mr. Zelks and Mr. Anderson telling the cap'n they thought we bent a propeller screw pretty good. That's why we're tilting a tad to starboard right now 'stead of being level."

"So it doesn't matter that it got bent?"

"Oh, it matters. We'll feel it on the surface. And when we want to get up some speed. We gotta figure how to fix it. But I don't guess now is the time."

Click . . . BAAAMM! Click . . . BAAAMM! Click . . . BAAAMM!

The radio on the wall jostled violently and tumbled from its hinges; chunks of cork insulation popped off the bulkhead like popcorn. The games cabinet jarred open, spraying them with dice and cards.

Nick began to look more alert now. He shook his head as if just waking up, then said, "They sure do make a clatter, don't they?"

Owen and Smitty stared at Nick: Nick, who never said anything funny, suddenly had said the goofiest thing and didn't even know it. Here they were, bombs blowing up all around them, and what they absolutely had to do was laugh. Smitty's lips twitched and his belly began to bounce. Owen tried to swallow a laugh, but it just came out as a hiccup. Nick blinked at them, as if suddenly realizing it was funny. Then Owen, Smitty and finally Nick, all exploded with laughter before remembering to cram a fist into their mouths to keep quiet.

Then came a terrible, metallic *P – I – N – G!* that echoed all around the *Mako*, like some giant pounding on a pipe. It froze

Owen, Nick, and Smitty, stopping the blood in their veins. The Japanese were zeroing in on their location—methodically, skillfully—trying to pinpoint them by echo searching in the ocean's depths. Any noise any of them made could be detected, and lethally dangerous.

Click . . . BAAAMM! Click . . . BAAAMM! Click ... BAAAMM!

Another string. Closer this time. The lights blinked. Owen felt a gust of air, and an instant later, his cheek throbbed like Pop hitting him, only—it was nothing like Pop's fist. It was dozens of tiny swords, but how could that be? As he reached for his cheek Smitty said in a commanding whisper:

"Don't touch it. Gallagher 'n' me'll tug the glass bits out."

Glass. So it was a shattered lightbulb. He noticed the room was dimmer. It seemed sensible to Owen that something like this should have happened, after all the tension and noise. It wasn't a war wound or anything—it just hurt. He was glad to have this to think on instead of listening to the Japanese trying to exact their revenge.

Click . . . BAAAMM! Click . . . BAAAMM! Click . . . BAAAMM! Click . . . BAAAMM! Click . . . BAAAMM!

Owen counted them off. There were more than before. He felt the *Mako* dip her nose down, off to port. Owen shrunk into himself and clutched at Smitty's arm.

"Smitty! Did they get us this time?" Owen's eyes searched Smitty's face. He was confused seeing Smitty softly chuckle and shake his head.

"Get us? Naw! That skipper. And Mr. Zelks. Found us a blanket to creep under."

"A what?"

TEMPERATURE GRADIENTS

Like land, the oceans have weather systems.
For example, when a sea meets an ocean, it
can set up an odd chopping wave pattern as
the currents attempt to mesh. Hot springs and
seasonal warmings create layers of different
underwater temperatures. Some submarines
in World War II had the specific mission to
chart these "blankets" so that their companion
vessels would know where to find them in
case of need. Many, however, were uncharted,
and the submariners during a depth charging
would keep their eyes glued to a device called
a bathothermograph. This measures the
compression and temperature of the water
surrounding the submarine and would alert
them that they were entering a zone with a
different temperature. Sonar from the surface
cannot accurately track through these gradients
and thus the submarine seems to "disappear";
the pings will deflect off the warm layer, rather
than off the submarine, disguising its true
position.

"A blanket. You know. Cap'n waited for a good string of ash cans to cover up the noise of diving deeper and gettin' under it. Sonar searching don't work good through a blanket. Bends the sound waves all nutty like."

"You mean—we'll be able to give them the slip?"

But it was Nick who answered this time. "Aww, Pasquerly. I know you didn't finish sub school, but you gotta know a temperature change down here is mighty good news for us."

The *Click . . . BAAAMMS!* got more muffled and further apart. They'd confused their pursuers. Nick and Smitty carefully pulled the glass shards from Owen's face. They sat together another two full hours with no more ash cans. Then Owen heard air roar into the ballast tanks, pushing the ocean's water out. He felt the *Mako* point her bow up to the surface: wobbling and tilting, but upward.

Up to fresh air, and another day to live.

L O C A T I O N: On the Surface, South
China Sea
Raff Abbott
From under the Sea

Raff had just enough energy left after the battle and depth charging to wave at his photo of Liz and the baby before staggering into his bunk. It was probably dumb, but he always blew a kiss at the picture frame bolted to his bedstand before he slept. He reached one arm out to peel off his scorched, smoky shirt—reeking with the smells of flame and close gunfire—but let it fall limp instead. *Sleep. I just care about sleep now.*

Raff's sleep was deep, dark, and unconscious as the deepest ocean trench, before rising up into a troubled dream. He was trying to say the name of the submarine that used to be his, but he couldn't remember. Smitty was there, opening and closing his mouth with the name, but Raff couldn't hear it. He knew if he couldn't say it they would die. Raff tossed and sweated until he startled awake, bolting up in bed.

Raff leapt from his bunk, pushed aside his curtained door, then ran down the corridor to the radio shack, nearly knocking Owen down and bursting a bag of flour.

"Sparks! Any word yet from the *Oarfish?*"

The Oarfish! He'd said the name.

Sparks sat surrounded by a wall of radio gadgetry. "Not a peep, Cap'n. I've been hailing her since we surfaced, but there's nothing yet. I expect she's still under, taking a pounding from that convoy, if she didn't get them all."

Raff felt his breath slowing down. *Of course. She's silent running. Can't receive or send messages submerged.* He heard Smitty's iron skillet banging on the stove and glanced at his watch. It was nearly 7 a.m. He'd slept for four hours. Long enough. What he needed more than sleep was to talk to Smitty. He knew Smitty would be taking a break soon. He poked his head into the galley and asked, "Smitty, when you get a minute, stop by my quarters, would you?"

"You got it, Cap'n," replied Smitty.

Raff lingered. "Smitty—did I ever mention? I'm glad you signed on with me again."

Smitty looked away a moment, then gazed directly at his skipper. "Wouldn't a missed it for the world, Cap'n."

Raff sat on his bunk, offering Smitty his desk stool. He knew they could be interrupted at any moment with some situation requiring his attention: an enemy plane sighted, damage reports from the battle, a MAGIC coded message. A hundred different things. And Smitty had to get back to cooking. But Smitty was the only guy he could talk to about this.

"Smitty, I've got a bad feeling about the *Oarfish.*"

Smitty stared at Raff, then shook his head. "Naw, Cap'n. *Oarfish*'s fine. Just getting' a pounding someplace. You know how it goes. You dish it out, you gets it back. Then you come up and do it again."

Raff clenched his jaw. "I suppose you're right. Still. I got a feeling."

"But they're a *fish*,' Cap'n! Everybody knows you're fine if you're a *fish*. Ain't never but one 'fish' sub sunk this whole war. You're just antsy 'cause you used to be her skipper."

"I suppose that's all it is," said Raff. He was about to ask Smitty if he still thought about their old *Oarfish* mates when Charlie Zelks knocked at the door panel and pulled open the curtain.

"We're running into wreckage, sir. From the convoy. There are some survivors. Do you want to take prisoners?"

"Yes. Two prisoners: that's regulation. I'm coming up."

Raff walked Smitty back to the galley. Raff still felt something was wrong with the *Oarfish*. Still, he knew Jake Jones was a good skipper, and there wasn't anything the *Mako* could do to help. Smitty was probably right.

Raff's sandals clicked on the metal rungs of the ladder to the bridge, his brain moving ahead of his body to picture how he'd deal with survivors. He couldn't save them all.

The official reason to take prisoners was to learn any scraps of news from them about Japanese strategy, movement of troops, or convoy whereabouts. But he was grateful also for any chance to save a life. It was a grim business. Kill and be killed.

Paul Anderson was waiting on deck. He said nothing—just pointed into the distance. Chunks of what used to be wooden hatches or furnishings bobbed chaotically on the white-capped waves. Raff grabbed Al Kaluza's binoculars to look at the blackened shapes that clung to the debris. They were human beings. Eight or ten of them, some suffering from wounds or shock: all of them coated in oil.

Raff felt a wave of pity and horror. *What am I going to do with them?* But he knew the answer.

"Let's get closer. Ahead, slow. Prepare life rings and inflate a raft," he ordered.

Three of them, upon seeing the American submarine, frantically waved their arms, signaling to keep away. He saw their expressions change from suffering, to dread, and then, to despair. Seeing the submarine come closer, they released hold of their chunks of wood—and began to drown.

"Have they gone cracked? They let go!" Paul gasped. "Wouldn't you want to take any chance you could?"

Raff shook his head. He didn't like to judge how someone else saw things, but he felt a kinship, an understanding for this act. Loyalty and duty make people do things contrary to what we would call our instincts. They may have felt this was the most honorable end. Or, perhaps some knew secrets they didn't want to fall into American hands.

"We could squeeze them all in. I'll get more life rings." Paul swung around.

Raff held his shoulder. "No. We've got switches and gears everywhere on this boat. Regulations are there for a reason. Two prisoners." Raff replied more harshly than he meant. He had to be harsh.

"You mean—they might sabotage?"

Raff nodded. "We'll have our hands full guarding two as it is."

"Permission to bring up the guns, sir?!"

Raff, startled, turned to see Buzz Gretz, his eyes glittering, his mouth set in a cruel smirk.

"Guns?" asked Raff.

SURVIVORS

British, German, Japanese—and American—
submarine captains sometimes acted with
appalling cruelty, machine-gunning and ramming
floating survivors. There are also documented
instances of the opposite, where an American
captain stopped his crew from shooting at
helpless men in the water.

"'Little target practice! Bag us some fresh Japs!'"

Fury coursed through Raff's blood. Through gritted teeth he snarled, "Not on my boat! Get below—get out of here!"

The *Mako* drew up alongside the wreckage. One of the figures beckoned to them. "Throw him a life ring," commanded Raff. So he'd be one prisoner. He wanted rescuing. But a second?

"Toss another ring in the middle," ordered Raff.

The ring flew into the air and bounced onto the water. Nothing happened for a moment. Raff wondered if they assumed they'd be tortured if they came on board—that was common practice the Japanese took toward prisoners.

Then one guy, in a decisive swoop, grabbed for it. A group of 4to8s pulled the two prisoners in and guided them up the curved hull onto the bridge. Raff watched their movements. He could learn a lot just by watching people. The safety of the *Mako* and her crew depended on it. The first cowered and staggered, as if he was scared and maybe also sick. The other exuded defiance, yanking himself away from the touch of the sailors who'd pulled him up.

"Paul, separate the prisoners. One in each torpedo room. That energetic one—chain his hands and feet. The other's not going to be a problem. Give them both food and water. Get Doc's help to swab that oil off their skins and see if they need medical attention."

He turned next to Chief Itty, who stood—greasy and sweaty—waiting to speak. "Repairs completed on the bent screw, sir. It was a mite tricky, but we got 'er."

"Good," replied Raff. Then, to Charlie: "Get ready to dive the boat. We need to leave here now."

Raff descended the ladder into the conning tower, then

into the control room, ready to give the command to leave the area—and the doomed sailors—behind. He thought to himself again what he'd told his crew: *People die out here. We shoot at them. They shoot at us.* It was simple, in a way. Maybe we live, maybe they live.

Maybe the *Mako* would be joining the *Oarfish* before long. And that was probably at the bottom of the South China Sea.

L O C A T I O N: Morning, under the South
China Sea
Enrique Romero
Prisoner in the Forward Torp Room

Enrique knew how to sleep through noise. Except for the noises
no submariner sleeps through: the klaxon sounding a dive, or
the chimes for battle stations. And depth charging. Nobody
could sleep through that.

He'd stirred from his morning shut-eye time to hear the
klaxon, and the good sound of the motor grinding as the
bow planes dipped to guide the boat down. Tom's dumb
wheewheewhee snores, and the 4to8s banging around doing
torpedo maintenance. All was well.

He may have slept awhile, or it may have been just a few
minutes later that he felt shaking at his side. He groaned and
opened his eyes the smallest amount possible.

"Enrique! Wake up!" Owen hissed into his ear as he yanked
at his elbow. "There's a Jap in here!"

Enrique jangled awake, flailing his arms and legs and
straining to see.

Mr. Anderson was crouched over something. A chain
dangled from a leg. Enrique heard little *clinkclink* noises as

it moved, then the sound of a key turning. He saw a pair of scrawny feet twisting in the shadows, under the sink, at the end of the forward torp room.

Enrique gripped the edge of his bunk and stared. There was a movement, then light fell onto the hands being chained together—and suddenly the edge of a face showed in the shadows. *A Jap face.* An angry eye looked defiantly at his captors before he slammed himself against the sink pipes.

"OK, listen up," said Mr. Anderson in a loud voice. He paused until everyone turned his way.

"All right, then. We've taken two prisoners. They'll be interrogated when we get to our base in Australia. This one's hostile: that's why he's being chained. But, you'll have me to answer to—and the captain—if he's not decently treated."

Enrique was sure Mr. Anderson wasn't soft on a Jap. What was this "decently treated" talk?

"We don't know his name, or what he may try to do, but expect an attempt at sabotage." Owen gasped at the word "sabotage." Enrique felt his pulse quicken and his brain race. Maybe he could catch this dirty Jap trying to mess with the *Mako:* the Jap would get executed, and he'd be a hero.

"There aren't any controls under the sink for him to mess with, so here he stays. Feed and toilet him every watch. Unchain just his feet to walk him through the boat for exercise. You're going to trip over him every time you brush your teeth or go for a pit stop. Every time you walk out of this door to the rest of the sub. Fifty times a day. So get used to it."

Mr. Anderson tossed a pillow from an empty bunk to the prisoner. He looked at each of them: Owen, Nick, Enrique, Tom, Eddie, Sparks, and Billy, then turned to Enrique.

"I expect you to act like a sailor, Romero," he said, placing the key in Enrique's hand before leaving.

"Why did he give it to you?" whispered Owen.

"Why not to me?" snapped Enrique, the key burning into his palm.

"Well—you're not on watch now," answered Owen, as if searching for a good reason.

"Yeah, that's true," said Billy, who was one of the 4to8s. "Maybe one of us should have the key."

"Shut up. I got the key. This Jap gets no walking around or pit stops until next watch. Or later." He glared at his friends.

Slowly, one by one, the fellows went back to their bunks, still staring at the hunched-up figure of the prisoner.

Enrique went back to his bunk, but not to sleep. From over the metal rim, he could see the prisoner's back. The prisoner turned, swiveling his bony, close-shaven head up. He spun further around, his chain stretching as far as it would go. He gazed contemptuously at the bunks before him. Then he met Enrique's eyes.

The prisoner's eyes flared like fire, then glowed with intensity at Enrique. His mouth twisted, and he muttered fierce-sounding words that sounded to Enrique like a curse. And Enrique glowered back, a low sound rumbling up from his chest, into a curse of his own.

It was like looking into a mirror. The Jap hated Enrique as much as he hated the Jap.

PRISONERS

It wasn't unusual for a pair of prisoners to be picked up by American subs to be questioned by interpreters in Australia for any information they might have on Japanese war plans or new equipment. Patronizing names and practical jokes (at the prisoners' expense) were likely, but prisoners weren't tortured or abused. Most sailors took the attitude "the war's over for this guy," although there were incidents of mutual hostility.

L O C A T I O N: Afternoon and Evening: On
and under the South China Sea
Raff Abbott
The Oarfish

Oarfish from Mako. Oarfish from Mako . . . S512 from S582 . . .
S512 from S582 . . . Come in, please . . .

Raff stood in the narrow doorway of the radio shack,
hovering over Sparks. They'd surfaced, even though it was the
middle of the afternoon in enemy waters, to try again to reach
their wolfpack partner. Nothing.

Raff wore a spare set of headphones, pushing the cups
hard into his ears, as if he could pick up a whisper, some tiny
sound, from his old submarine. He stared at the dials in front
of Sparks, mentally commanding a response. *Oarfish! Oarfish!*
Come in, please!

Smitty appeared at the door with coffee for Raff and Sparks.
His forehead was fixed in a crease, showing more puzzlement
than fear. Raff glanced over at Smitty, saw him silently mouth,
"A 'fish,' Cap'n. She's a 'fish.' "

Raff realized that Smitty put great stock in the fact that
only one of the submarines sunk thus far in the war had been a
"fish"—even though many U.S. submarines were named "fish."

Raff knew submarines inside and out: knew how they were built, knew how they could meet their end. A plane might drop a bomb or shoot her full of holes. They could hit a mine—or catch a depth charge. He visualized the *Oarfish*, not because he wanted to, but because he could not stop it. In some compartment—perhaps it would be the after engine room—the crew would have a split second of realization that the four-inch steel hull had been breached. Water roars in with inconceivable force. They will be the first to die.

Almost immediately, the sub upends, tossing everything not bolted down against what used to be the bulkhead. Sailors ignore the pain of their eardrums, ruptured from the intense pressure, and clamber onto mess tables, bunks, and ladder rungs to escape the water. The depth gauges in the control room spin wildly; the ones that still work pass the red danger arrow and keep dialing up until they jam. The watertight doors cannot hold for long. It is too deep to attempt an escape using the Momsen lung. There are some prayers; some fellows hold on to one another. There are groans, human and from the metal of the *Oarfish* warping and collapsing.

Down she goes, down and down, until the keel whips apart and the ribbing screeches and twists, then gives way. The steel hull collapses. Eighty sailors go down to the bottom of the sea.

From somewhere far off, Raff heard a call: "Cap'n! Captain Abbott!" He pulled off the headphones, then turned to see Charlie, slowly noticing the *Mako's* klaxon had sounded its *AhOOOOgah! AhOOOOgah!* diving alert.

"Couldn't stay up any longer, Captain. We sighted a plane. Looked like a Betty bomber."

"All right, then. Carry on."

"BETTY" BOMBER

Different types of Japanese planes were given female nicknames by the Americans. The "Betty" was a particularly prevalent, and feared, bomber. The Mitsubishi G4M had two 1,530-horsepower engines. It could travel 265 miles per hour and carry two 1,765-pound bombs and depth charges, as well as three 7.7 mm guns and a 20 mm cannon.

Behind Charlie, Raff saw the anxious faces of Enrique and Nick. "Did you get through to the *Oarfish?*" asked Gallagher.

They have someone on the Oarfish, too, Raff remembered. *Dave Baine was one of their sub school teachers.* He shook his head, then said, "We're nearly at the intersection point of the *Oarfish's* last known course. When it gets dark, we'll come up again and keep trying to hail them."

Romero and Gallagher looked like they wanted him to say something more: something to reassure them. Raff could have given them a nod, a smile, to ease them. But he did not lie to his crew. Not ever.

"Surface the boat, sir? Sonar reports all is quiet above," asked the 4to8 diving officer. They had been submerged most of the day. Darkness was falling. Charlie would want to get a star fix to be sure they were in the right area to find the *Oarfish*.

"Take her up," said Raff. "And somebody get Gallagher. I'll need those eyes of his tonight." He wanted to find out the truth about the *Oarfish*, whatever it was.

Raff heard all the normal sounds of a healthy submarine surfacing. The methodical repeating of orders as sailors checked valves and adjusted their instruments. The whoosh and whistle of high-pressure air shoving walls of water out of the tanks. He felt the *Mako* becoming buoyant as they lifted up to the surface.

"Open main induction!" came the diving alert. The *whap-clunk* of the induction valve opening, now drawing air from the surface, allowed the switch from battery power to engines. The throaty bass of the diesel engines rumbled through the *Mako*, forming its odd duet with the screechy blower in the pump room, which was finishing emptying water from the ballast tanks. Now the diesels connected to the generators and began the task of powering up the batteries.

Charlie carried the sextant topside to take their position. Raff stood by his side, grateful for the clear night and the brilliant canopy of stars in the dusky sky. Charlie would be able to tell almost exactly where they were from what four dazzling stars could tell him.

"You'd never know that just two nights ago there was a big battle not far from here," said Charlie to Raff, putting the sextant back into its case. "And maybe," he added, "it was right about here that the *Oarfish* got some good shots off at what we didn't get of the convoy."

Raff flinched at the words "right about here." Had the *Oarfish* been here? Did she finish off what was left of the convoy? If she had, why couldn't the *Mako* pick up some sign of her?

"Keep a sharp eye out, Gallagher. Watch the surface close in to us. Not the far horizon tonight. Tell me anything strange you see," ordered Raff.

Raff knew what he was looking for. It wouldn't be easy to see. That's why he needed Gallagher.

It was only a little while later that Nick said, "Cap'n? You said to tell you about anything strange. I don't think this could be any kind of marine life . . ."

"What is it?"

"It looks like rainbows on the water. Rings of rainbow."

Raff gripped the edge of the splash shield. In a tight voice, he ordered the engines to stop. It was a long two or three minutes before Raff could make out what Gallagher had seen all too clearly.

Rainbows, spreading out in a circle. Beautiful rainbows bouncing on the waves marked the grave of the *Oarfish*. A little bit of oil would have escaped when they were bombed and risen to make this pattern. There would be nothing else. Nothing for the enemy to capture and examine. No secrets given up.

Perhaps the *Oarfish* did sink something before getting sunk. Raff could not officially declare the *Oarfish* lost until after it had again missed the 1:00 a.m. check-in time. But in the marrow of his bones, Raff knew they would miss it.

It was a lucky break—or perhaps it was grace, a blessing—that he didn't need to make an announcement until then. Except for telling one man. The *Mako* would be in the hands of his officers and crew for a while. Now, he must find Smitty. Then he would go to his compartment for a short while, to be alone.

L O C A T I O N: On the South China Sea
Owen Pasquerly
Hailing Dead Men

Smitty said the galley belonged to him in the daytime, then at
night it was Owen's territory. Regular and predictable as the
turning of the earth. Owen was used to it now. He slept in the
daytime. Smitty slept at night. But not last night. Or tonight.

The peaceful feeling Owen usually had as he formed his
loaves and smelled them baking didn't come tonight. He felt
like a piece of elastic pulled too tight and held stretched hour
after hour.

Something bad was going to happen. Or maybe it already
had. Smitty kept pacing back and forth between the radio
shack and the galley. Sometimes he muttered to himself. Owen
didn't know if he should pretend nothing was happening.

"What did you say, Smitty? I didn't quite catch that," said
Owen, finally.

Smitty stared at Owen as if he just became aware there was
someone else nearby. Smitty was supposed to be cranky and
unflappable. But now his face looked all wrong.

Owen felt like the elastic snapped loose and whipped at
him.

Smitty blinked hard, then said: "She's a 'fish,' ya see. The *Oarfish*. 'Fish' don't get sunk. They've got the luck. It's right in 'er name. Cap'n can't be right. Can't be right." He shook his head and started for the radio shack again.

Smitty had told Owen, back on that first day, that he was a loner. But his huge shoulders sagged now, and he looked like he needed something. Smitty was the other half of himself on the *Mako*. They kept the guys fed. It wasn't being in on the action. But the action couldn't happen without what they did: cooking and baking, mixing and stirring.

"Let's go see Sparks," Owen said, hopefully. "Maybe he can raise a signal." Owen draped his arm over Smitty's back. Smitty let Owen steer him down the corridor.

Oarfish from Mako. Oarfish from Mako. Come in, please.

Sparks's voice was hoarse. Owen glanced at the clock. It was just past 1:00 a.m. Why wasn't the captain there? He always was in the radio shack for check-in time with their wolfpack partner.

"They gotta be there, Sparks!" said Smitty. "Maybe yer doing the wrong signal?"

"I've checked and rechecked it," Sparks panted. "It's our signal. What we've always used. *S512 from S582 . . . Come in, please . . . Oarfish from Mako. Come in, please.*"

"Then try *another* signal." Smitty's voice was begging.

"It's the only signal we can use. The only one there is," snapped Sparks. "I've been hailing for hours. I got friends on that boat."

"I know. Yer doing yer best."

Owen stared at the walls of speakers and receivers and flashing lights surrounding Sparks, as if they could reach out to

. . . But before he could finish the thought, a chill gripped his insides—*to dead men.*

Sparks kept hailing. Perhaps for half an hour. Perhaps longer. Owen was held in a circle of fear and hope, with Smitty and Sparks.

Gradually, Owen became aware of the captain next to them.

"Take the headphones off, Sparks."

Sparks startled, clutched at the headphones, then slowly slid them down his face onto his lap.

"It's time to stop. They're gone. Let them rest."

The captain's words made a sound rise up in Smitty's chest. A stifled sob that expanded and sank. At that moment, Owen knew there are no loners on a submarine.

Owen couldn't feel as they did about the crew of the *Oarfish.* He hadn't met them. But Smitty, Sparks, the captain, and the others of the *Mako*—they were his people, his tribe. He would give them coffee and bread. It was not much, but it was what he had. What made the rest of it possible: the fighting, the living, the carrying on.

L O C A T I O N: On the South China Sea
Nick Gallagher
Warriors

"That's it? They're just *gone?*" asked Eddie, of nobody in particular. The 12to4s, with Owen, shuffled one at a time into the forward torpedo room. It was 4:30 in the morning.

"It seems unreal. We traded movies with those guys," said Owen, punching at his bunk pillow. He glared at the Japanese prisoner hunched up under the sink.

"And Lieutenant Baine. He was here joking around with us. Right here . . . ," added Eric, pointing at the spot by the forward tubes.

"Say, Gallagher," began Eddie, "when you saw those oil rings, you knew they'd gone down, right?"

Nick shook his head. "I didn't know. Those rainbow rings . . . I knew they upset the captain. But he didn't say why. Guess he wanted to keep hoping we'd get a radio response or something before giving up."

"Well, they're on eternal patrol now," said Sparks solemnly.

They all nodded and were silent. Then Enrique leapt up from his bunk, pouncing on the prisoner. He kicked and punched at the bound man. "Filthy Jap! Killer! Murderer!" he screamed.

ETERNAL PATROL

"Eternal patrol" is the phrase used by submariners to honor their dead companions. It means the war patrol never ends for them, and they've gone to a place of rest. The casualty rate in the submarine service was the highest for any branch of the Navy in World War II. One in five sailors, or 20 percent, did not survive. Almost every submariner vividly remembers buddies who died during a battle, or from depth charging or from hitting a mine.

The others stared, transfixed. Slowly, they gathered themselves, moving as one toward the prisoner, who was spitting and yelling back at Enrique. Nick felt his will leave his body as he merged with the others, circling in for the attack.

Then, the face of Lieutenant Baine flickered across his mind. He was pointing with that pencil of his. What was it? What had he said? *You've got a job to do. You're warriors. Not butchers.*

Nick flung his arms out between the 12to4s and the prisoner. Panting, he cried: "Stop! We've got to stop it!"

Somebody paused; it might have been Owen. Then somebody else gave one more kick and stopped. Was it Tom? But there was still shoving and kicking and shouting as the prisoner was rammed again and again against the bulkhead. Nick found a voice that was a command. It came loud and deep:

"That's enough! He wouldn't like it!"

They staggered back. Enrique snarled, "What are you talking about! That guy killed everybody!"

"He didn't kill everybody. Yeah, the Japs started this. And we're getting them back. But we can't like this."

Enrique's face went red, and his fists were clenched. "Get out of my way, Nicky." Nick kept talking—faster, to get Enrique to listen. "He's dead now. I can't explain, but he wouldn't want us doing this. We owe him that. Lieutenant Baine, I mean," said Nick, looking from one to the other of his friends, while dimly aware that the prisoner's yells had turned to moans.

They listened to Nick, as they always did. Looked up to him, though Nick never understood why. Nick kept talking.

"He said we were warriors, remember? Warriors, not butchers. He said that. We've got to be . . . I don't know the right words. I just know what he meant. Yeah, we torpedo their ships. But this guy isn't in it now. Heck, he's got his feet and hands chained. Yeah, he hates us. We blew up his ship. I bet he had buddies, like we've got buddies. Even . . ." He turned hesitantly to Enrique, as the words found their way out: "I don't know . . . even maybe a . . . cousin."

That last word came out soft, for Enrique to hear without the hurt of Juan crushing down on him. But Nick saw that the softness made it worse, saw Enrique's eyes grow big and wild. Enrique made a gulping sound, then bolted from the room. Owen stared at Nick, began to say, "Why'd you have to . . . ?" then ran after Enrique.

One by one, the others made their way back to their bunks. It was roomier now that some of the torpedoes had been fired.

They felt the *Mako* on the surface. She was full of energy, more like a dolphin skimming the waves than her shark namesake. Nick wondered if their submarine was saying, "It'll be all right. I'll do the battles. See how sleek I am?"

There was silence for a few minutes. Then Eddie asked, "Does anybody know what Lieutenant Baine did on the *Oarfish?*"

Sparks answered, "I know he ran the TDC."

"I can just see him up there in the conning tower," Tom chimed in, "dialing the settings, twirling the dials to get it right. He probably helped get off some good shots at that convoy . . ."

Before they got him, was the unspoken thought hanging in the air.

"You suppose they went down fast?" asked Eddie, a catch in his voice.

Nick didn't know the answer, but he wanted to believe what he said: "It was probably pretty fast. One of those depth charges that just hit square."

Nick saw, in his mind's eye, his old teacher with eyes closed, tranquil and at peace, at the bottom of the green-blue South China Sea.

L O C A T I O N: Topside on the U.S.S. Mako
Nick Gallagher
Pearl Necklace

Nick walked slowly, and wobbled as he made his way toward his lookout post. His head was tipped back. He stared up at the velvety black night with its net of white stars. A shooting star dripped molten white speckles across the eastern sky. It seemed to pulsate with life and mystery. It was the loveliest night Nick had ever seen.

"Nice night, eh, Gallagher?" asked Mr. Anderson.

"It sure is something," agreed Nick, hoisting himself up the periscope shears. He tapped Eric's shoulder to signal that he was there to relieve him, then took the binoculars. Nick leaned his elbows on the support ring and surveyed the sky and sea. What was left of the convoy had vanished, and there was no sign of any other ships.

Nick was keeping watch, but his eyes could work while his mind wandered. Everything always felt so open and enormous coming topside, after being in the submarine. But tonight he felt tiny and almost weightless, as if he could be blown away on the breeze and float up into the glittery sky.

The stars were never this bright at home.

His thoughts floated out through the oval view of the binoculars. He thought of the fields at home, and how they smelled on a fall night. He thought, too, of Enrique, who'd been avoiding him since yesterday morning's argument about the prisoner.

The *Mako* was in waters with flying fish again, but not so shallow this time. Through the binocs he saw them leap up. It was like fireflies and sparklers wherever a flying fish, or the *Mako*'s own wake, disturbed the surface.

It was hard to believe there was a war on. Hard to believe the *Oarfish* had been sunk. Hard to believe that he'd ever been up on deck with Japanese guns blasting and smoking all around him.

Hey, what's that?

Nick's eyes locked onto something unfamiliar, and his mind focused quickly on what was in the binocs. In a few seconds, he could make out the squared-off sails of fishing boats.

"Sampans! Off the port bow," he called out.

"I've got some off to starboard, too!" yelled Eddie. "Three or four of 'em."

"This is probably great fishing territory, so I'm not surprised," replied Mr. Anderson. "They must be Chinese. Anchored for the night."

Nick relaxed.

The smell of Owen's freshly baked bread came wafting up the open hatch. It was mouth watering. The 12to4s always got first crack at Owen's baked goodies.

Nick felt a tap on his shoulder. His twenty-minute rotation was up. Time for a relief. It was Tom Benson's turn; Nick was due to assist in the conning tower.

With his binoculars down, the night again seemed huge and seemed to lift him up. Nick spun around. Millions of glittery white specks glowed down on him, like pearls. He wanted to gather them up and give them to someone. To who?

To Mom, he thought. *Yeah, that's it. Mom would like this.*

He imagined his mother reaching her hand up toward her throat. It was her habit when she worried to stroke at her throat. Was she missing him? Worried about him?

What if he gave her the surprise of her life? What if, when she reached up, she stopped looking worried and smiled a big, bright smile? Smiled because she'd be stroking a fine pearl necklace.

The stars and the shimmering water had given him an idea. He knew there were villages in Australia that fished for pearls. When they went on leave, he could buy a necklace.

But he'd ask Enrique to help him pick it out. Enrique knew more than he did about women.

L O C A T I O N: Under and on the South
China Sea
Owen Pasquerly
Guns and Bread

Back home in Montana, Owen would still be sleeping at 4 a.m.
On the *Mako*, not only was he wide awake, but this had come
to be his favorite time of day.

The galley—his galley—was the heart of the boat now. His
bread sat cooling on the racks, together with pies or whatever
else he'd decided to make. Delicious smells drew hungry sailors
his way. It felt good to see his 12to4 friends come off watch and
eat what he'd made.

This morning started off like all the rest.

"You should have seen it topside, Owen," said Nick, as he sat
down at his favorite spot. "The stars are amazing up there."

"Quiet watch, then?"

"Yup. Except for seeing some Chinese fishing boats," said
Eddie, answering for Nick.

"How do you know they're Chinese?"

"Mr. Anderson told us," said Enrique, who was the last one
to come off watch.

Suddenly, Eddie whispered "Pssst," and tipped his thumb

toward the corridor. Captain Abbott was walking slowly past, absorbed in reading a message.

"I'll bet that's a MAGIC message. Secret," said Eddie. "Hey, Owen. Did you see Sparks talking with the Old Man?"

"Nope. But Sparks usually stays in the radio shack, so I don't see who he's talking to," Owen replied. "If it—" But the captain's voice on the intercom interrupted him.

"All hands. This is the captain. I've received an intelligence report that the Japanese have taken over some civilian boats. One of the sampans sighted by the 12to4s has separated from the others. We're going to follow it under water, then surface and check it out. Mr. Anderson will lead the investigative party. He'll need a volunteer or two to assist with gunnery. Captain out."

"Those boats didn't look like anything," said Nick.

"Could be they're swarming with spies," said Enrique.

"Well, I'm going to find out!" said Owen, running out of the galley.

Mr. Anderson was slowly adjusting his cap when Owen found him in the corridor outside the officers' quarters. He had changed into his full dress uniform.

"Mr. Anderson! Permission to join the gun detail?" Owen burst out.

"Join them? This might turn into a combat situation. You haven't been trained on guns."

"I'm a good shot, sir. You know I am," Owen persisted.

"Pasquerly, listen to me. If that's a spy boat—and that's what I've got to find out—they could have a machine gun. They'll be cornered and maybe desperate. We won't fire unless they do, but there could be a lot of bullets flying around. I'd be the first to be killed. But I might not be the only one."

Owen flinched. But he replied, "I still want to, sir."

"All right then. Take a rifle. But you have to stay to the rear of the other gunners, understood?"

"Yes, sir."

Owen walked with Mr. Anderson into the forward torpedo room, joining Buzz and Ace, who looked grim and edgy. He heard, "Surface! Surface!" over the intercom and felt the bow pointing up.

The *Mako* crashed through the surface. The hatch swung open. The water hadn't fully drained off the bridge; thin streams of it cascaded down on Owen's head. Mr. Anderson leapt up the ladder, closely followed by the gunners.

Owen felt a strange curiosity. This could be his first battle. He'd get off a good shot. Maybe he'd kill somebody. If they shot him, what would it be like? Would he feel like his whole body was on fire, and not even know where the pain was coming from? Or would he hear only a zing in the air—like a hummingbird—then notice warm, spurting blood?

There it was. Bobbing back and forth wildly on waves churned up by the *Mako*'s rise from the sea. Standing behind Mr. Anderson and the other gunners, Owen saw a small boat. He raised his rifle.

Sails hung stained and threadbare. A dozen guys in sandals and ragged T-shirts stared up at Mr. Anderson—then shifted their gaze to the *Mako*'s guns pointed at their hearts. They stood motionless, rigid with terror. The only sounds were the *thump-slug* of waves against the submarine and the whispery breeze around them.

Is this the start of a battle? Is it quiet like this? wondered Owen.

Mr. Anderson stood at the edge of the *Mako* and leaned over to scan the fishing boat. Owen's finger tightened on the brass trigger of his gun.

"There's no radio in here. No weapons. Just fish and gear," Mr. Anderson called over his shoulder. Owen took his finger from the trigger, both relieved and disappointed that there wouldn't be a battle after all.

Mr. Anderson stepped back and signaled the gunners to put down their guns. "These guys are really fishermen," he said. He gave a little wave to let them know they were free to go. But no one moved. He waved again.

They didn't understand. Hand signals hadn't worked. No one knew the other's language.

Owen could see one guy begin to tremble so much he nearly fell over. *They think we're going to shoot them dead.*

A faint smell of fresh bread floated up the open hatch.

"Your bread, Pasquerly!" Mr. Anderson shouted. "Get me some!"

Startled, Owen scrambled back down the hatch and reappeared, holding a loaf.

Maybe the fishermen had never even eaten bread like that before, but seeing it held out toward them, in Mr. Anderson's outstretched hand, they understood:

It was a sign of peace.

The fishermen swiveled their boat around to nudge up next to the *Mako*. Owen and Ace and Buzz stepped around their guns to throw some ropes to the fishermen, who shimmied up on deck. They were sweaty, and they smelled of fish and sunshine and hard work.

Mr. Anderson pulled chunks off the loaf and gave them to the Chinese, then popped a corner of the crust into his own mouth. Owen went to get more bread, grinning as he returned with an armload.

"That bread of yours sure came in handy," said Mr. Anderson. "Light and peace. That's what we got today. What do you think of that?"

Owen looked up at the sky. It was a brilliant blue: the first daylight he had seen in three weeks.

The captain came on deck. "Paul," he said to Mr. Anderson, "remember where we are. If a plane spots us, we'll be sitting ducks. They need to leave now."

Mr. Anderson pointed to the fishing boat, then made a sweeping motion with his hand. They must have understood, because two of the fishermen held up their hands in a gesture that clearly meant, "Just a moment." They climbed down the rope into their boat, then reappeared, staggering under the weight of an immense basket of seafood.

A gift.

The fishing boat unfurled her sails and drifted away on top of the South China Sea. The *Mako* submerged under it, wrapped in shimmering blue water, then dissolving into the richer blue, then the black-blue depths.

Owen baked biscuits that evening to go with Smitty's fried squid, tuna, and clams. Some fresh beans or corn on the cob would have been nice, if anything like that had still been in the storerooms, but no one complained.

After the battles and the depth charges and the grieving they'd been through, light and peace were what they had on the *Mako* that day. Owen's bread had helped it happen. Ordinary old bread.

"All hands. This is the captain speaking."

Owen wiped his apron and switched off his mixing bowl to hear the announcement.

"I've just received new orders from ComSubPac. We're to detour south for lifeguard duty. Seems our zoomies will be conducting a raid near Singapore. If they get into trouble and need to splash down, we'll fish 'em out. But we're going to have to make flank speed to get there on time, so we'll be on the surface as much as we can. Expect frequent dives during daylight to avoid the Bettys. Captain out."

Rescuing fighter pilots! That was something new for the *Mako*. Owen thought about Gary, who might be in Europe, but what if he was right here, in the South China Sea?

It was nearly 9 p.m. Owen had started his night of baking an hour ago. He felt the *Mako* turn around, but it didn't climb to top speed. Owen wondered why not.

He'd ask Enrique about it when he wandered into the mess around 11:30 p.m. He always spent time chatting before starting his watch.

Owen checked on his bread to be sure it was rising properly. It struck him—suddenly—that he'd been baking bread, rolls, and other stuff for eighty fellows, since heading out to sea. *After the war is over, I could open up my own bakery. I don't need Pop. I'm good!*

The first batch of loaves was in the oven when Enrique, Eric, and Nick sauntered into the mess. All of them were wearing their red goggles for first rotation on lookout. Nick and Eric were yawning and stretching. But, as usual, Enrique was lively and flashing his famous grin.

"Bread! Ah! Yum!" he sighed, lifting his goggled head up into the air and hovering around the galley door.

"Not done yet, Romeo," sighed Owen. "You know they're never out this early."

Enrique looked crushed. His shoulders slumped. "Oh, geez."

"How about sugar doughnuts?" asked Nick.

"Nope, but . . ." Owen ducked down to the tiny refrigerator at his feet and pulled out a chocolate cream pie. That was easy to make since it didn't need to go into the oven: just mixing and chilling. He'd whipped it up before starting the bread.

"Here, you guys. I made this. Save some for Haverly and Benson, OK?"

"Pasquerly, you are a culinary genius," said Enrique, perking up. "That means you bake good."

"Hmm," said Nick, looking around. "We've picked up some speed. I can feel it."

"Say, did you guys sleep through the Old Man's announcement?" asked Owen.

"What announcement?" asked Eric, with a yawn.

"We're heading way south. Someplace near Singapore. We've got lifeguard duty to rescue zoomies," replied Owen.

"Yeah? That's out of our quadrant. They must really need us," said Eric.

Nick, normally serious and thoughtful, started to snicker.

"What is it, Nicky?" asked Enrique.

"Won't Haverly be mad he didn't get the word before we did?!"

They all laughed, picturing Eddie Haverly scowling and sniffing about being in the dark on hot news.

As the lookouts wolfed down the last of the pie, Owen asked, "How come we're not going flank speed right now, like Cap'n said we would?"

"Have to power up the battery at night, remember? Can't use all four engines now for speed. If we're diving and ducking from planes on the way, we'll need plenty of can," Eric replied.

"Can? Can of what?"

Enrique reached over the counter and yanked on Owen's apron. "Tut, tut, tut," he scolded. "Let's get the sailor talk down! 'Can' means battery power."

"Oh, yeah," mumbled Owen.

"So, Sparks. I've been wondering. Will a zoomie in trouble radio us, or how will we know where to find the guy?"

Enrique stood in the doorway of the radio shack talking to Sparks. The *Mako* had been en route since Tuesday, diving often during daylight to avoid Japanese planes. Now it was late Wednesday afternoon, and the first chance Enrique had had to ask.

"Oh, yeah, Romeo. Reports have been coming over radio since last night. We've got a call signal our guys can use if they need to, and we're getting the I.D. codes of each plane going on the raid."

"What's our signal going to be? A nickname or something?"

"Yeah, we got 'Fighting Shark.' Good one, don't you think?"

"That's our *Mako*," grinned Enrique.

That night the 12to4s got briefed on the rescue plan. All the lookouts for the watch, the officers, the gun crew, Sparks and the other radiomen, plus Doc in case a flyer was wounded, gathered in the control room. Buzz Gretz and Al Kaluza had been asked to be there, too, because they were especially big guys. If a flier was wounded, they could hoist him up onto the *Mako*.

The captain stood with his arms folded and a foot propped up on the ladder to the conning tower.

"OK, fellows. This is hot off the wires. We just got a coded message telling us the time of the raid. We've taken a pretty good pounding from the Japanese in the Philippines. Now it's payback time—and it's going to happen on your watch. Tomorrow afternoon, Thursday."

Enrique and the others whooped and clapped their hands.

The captain continued: "We can't expect to have no hits, but with luck, it'll just be airplanes that take some bullets. The zoomie can parachute out of a shot-down plane so the *Mako* can rescue.

"Of course, this is happening in daylight: our most vulnerable time. We'll wait to surface as long as possible. We've got a short-distance radio band set up so that we can stay submerged at periscope depth and still receive a distress signal. But I want gunners on the big guns standing ready in case there's a Betty nearby.

"Get whatever sleep you can before tomorrow afternoon. We'll do a drill tonight at 2 a.m. to get clear on the operation. Dismissed."

Everybody scattered like bowling pins, hurrying to tell the news—and to get ready for the drill. Enrique pivoted on his sandals to get to the forward torpedo room, but as he did, he glanced at the captain's face.

A line had appeared across his forehead, and an eyebrow dipped down.

Something was worrying the captain of the *Mako*.

L O C A T I O N: South China Sea
Enrique Romero
Rescue

"Fighting Shark! Fighting Shark! This is Utah Eight. Took a bullet in my wing. Will splash down near your position."

It was happening. They could hear the bombs of the air strike. And the guns of the Japanese.

Enrique jerked his head up as the distress call blared through the radio mounted on the mess bulkhead. He nearly slid off his tiny metal stool as he grabbed Nick's arm. They sat next to each other in the control room: Enrique on the stern planes and Nick on the bow planes.

Sparks ran into the control room and hollered up the ladder that a message had been received and that "Utah Eight" was a verified code word of a U.S. airplane.

Enrique's station at the stern planes control was almost directly below the ladder to the conning tower; he could hear everything.

"Up scope!" came the captain's voice. Immediately, a soft whirring sounded near Enrique as the periscope rose from its well at the base of the submarine to pierce the water's surface.

"I spot him! Looks like he's having trouble with that wing. Smoke plume coming from the rear. It's an F-6.

"Prepare to surface. Radio, alert Utah Eight we're on our way," said the captain.

AhOOOgah! AhOOOgah! The klaxon blared throughout the boat. Enrique felt the deck vibrate as the gunners and rescue team ran to the control room, ready to vault up the ladders.

Nick pulled in the bow planes as Enrique dipped out the stern planes, like a porpoise tipping and tilting its fins to ascend. They were down only sixty feet, so in moments Enrique felt the *Mako* crash through the water and level off, buoyant and bobbing on the waves.

As they'd practiced in their drills, the captain emerged first from the hatch, then three gunners, then Al Kaluza and Buzz Gretz. Nick quickly pulled his levers to rig out the bow planes in a locked position to use as a platform for the rescue. Enrique leapt up the ladder, Nick following, out the conning tower hatch. Enrique thrust one set of binoculars into Nick's chest and hung one around his own neck, as they climbed up to their lookout positions.

Just like in the drills. *So far so good,* thought Enrique.

Enrique and Nick, along with the gunners, had the job of watching the sky for any danger from above. They squinted into the dazzlingly bright sun. Enrique would have rather watched the rescue, but at least he could hear what was going.

"He's splashing. He's pulling back his canopy. Raft's inflating next to him." It was the captain's voice.

"Geez! Look at the steam coming up from that engine," said Buzz. Enrique always knew that voice.

Enrique kept scanning the sky. Nothing. He heard footsteps and a metallic groan. *Must be Gretz and Kaluza stepping on a bow plane to hoist the guy up.*

Then things moved very fast—or was it that they slowed down, but were too terrible to fit into reality.

"In the sky!" shouted Nick. "I think it's a Betty!" Enrique swung his binocs wildly around, but caught only piercing glare refracting on the glass. The *Mako's* machine guns blasted *DUT! DUT! DUT!* In the same instant Enrique heard a voice—was it the captain's?—"Get that zoomie down! Lookouts below! Dive! Dive!"

Enrique's binocs bounced onto his chest. He spun around as he let himself fall from his perch onto the bridge. He saw Kaluza and Gretz, right in front of him, push the flier down the hatch like a bag of laundry, then drop down themselves. In the next moment Enrique's foot reached for the top rung of the conning tower ladder, but someone shoved him and Enrique lost his footing. He vaulted head first down the hatch, managing to grab a rung and jerk his hip around to protect his head from crashing onto the floor. He felt a snap; his leg exploded with pain. Someone had landed on top of him, then someone else yanked both of them away from the path of the descending gunners and the captain.

AhOOOgah! AhOOgah! The klaxon sounded its warning; the *Mako* was already beginning its dive. In a pain-filled daze, half-lying on the conning tower floor, Enrique looked to see what was draped across his back. At the same moment his brain registered sounds of panting and sharp, thin cries.

It was Nick.

L O C A T I O N: South China Sea
Nick Gallagher
Hit

Bright sun. Bright sun. Can't see. Danger! Something silver. Flying. Coming at us!

   Fire in my chest. Ah! Ah! Put it out! Where's Romeo? Ah! Going to burn us up! Can't see. Can't see.

   Nicky! Nicky!

   Someone calling. Too hot. Inside me. Can't see.

   Don't move him. Get Doc up here.

   Ah! Ah! Too bright. In the sky! Look up! On fire. Here. Get it out. No, no, no.

   How bad, Doc?

   More than I can handle. Maybe if . . . in Australia. I'm going to give him something to ease the pain.

   Is it Dad? Dad? Our fields. They melted into waves. Waves, on and on. Then someone set them on fire. Put water on it. Yes, water, yes . . .

L O C A T I O N: South China Sea;
Midsection of the Mako
Owen Pasquerly
Supposing

Owen hovered behind the captain and Doc. He stared at his friends, now both asleep. Doc carefully moved Nick's arm to check the reddish brown bandage covering his chest. Disinfectant and strange body smells rose up from the place where Nick had been shot. Owen felt throw-up lurch into his throat. He swallowed it back.

"Has Gallagher regained consciousness?" asked the captain.

"In and out. Recognized Romero awhile ago. Then he drifted out again. That's when Romero finally fell asleep, too," Doc replied.

"You've been giving him morphine?"

Doc nodded.

"And Romero?"

"Got a clean break to his leg. He'll heal up."

"I've alerted ComSubPac. We're cutting the patrol short. Lucky thing we're this far south. We can get to base in a few days," said the captain.

"I don't know if even that's . . ." Doc trailed off as he darted a glance at Owen.

Owen shuddered. "What do you mean, Doc? The Aussies' got hospitals! More medicines than us, right?"

"Yes, they have all that." Doc opened his mouth like he was going to say something else, but instead went to refill the water bucket. Nick moaned and began to turn his head from side to side.

"I'll tell Smitty to cover for you. Stay here. With them," said the captain.

Owen nodded. He sat with his legs drawn up to his chin, on the floor between his friends. He listened to the quick, labored breath of Nick and the deeper breath of Enrique.

If they die, what happens to me? Other kids my age are playing baseball at home, and I'm watching my friends die. No. Not going to happen.

Owen sniffled and began to rock back and forth. He tried to think about what could make all this worth it.

Supposing that zoomie we saved is going to be somebody really important. Like a scientist who cures some terrible disease. Or president. Yeah, president of the United States. Then it would be . . . worth it?

But Owen couldn't believe that anything could make this worth it. He didn't know the zoomie or care what might happen someday. Right now, right here. Him and his friends. That was all that was real.

Stay alive. Stay alive. Stay alive.

LIFEGUARD DUTY

Rescuing downed fliers ("zoomies") was hazardous, but WWII submariners are proud to have saved over 550 American pilots who splashed into the Pacific. On September 2, 1944, the U.S.S. *Finback* changed the course of world events with the rescue of flier Lieutenant j.g. George Bush. Bush went on to become president of the United States, as did his son, George W. Bush.

Raff had to set aside his grief over the *Oarfish*'s sinking—and his worry about Nick Gallagher. Had to, because there was a war to fight. But he would also do everything in his power to get the *Mako* back home safely.

The cover of darkness was used up. He'd ordered the engines to be pushed hard all night to make headway to their base in Australia. Still, he took care to power up the batteries for running submerged. The *Mako* dove right after Charlie had taken their position at dawn. Speed slowed down as soon as they dove.

Now, it was 8 a.m. Time for a periscope check of the surface. The *Mako* was in new waters now. Out of the South China Sea and in the smaller Java Sea. Raff draped his arm over the periscope as it ascended and fitted his cheekbone into the eyepiece. He began to swivel the scope, ready to see the emptiness of water and sky.

Instead, the black outline of a ship, its stacks belching smoke, filled the circle of his viewfinder. An oil tanker! A priority target. He'd have to stop and get this one.

She was steering a straight course with no escorts. Raff tipped the periscope to see Bettys dotting the sky, but the setup was perfect for a quick shoot. Raff called out, "Battle stations!" The alarm rang throughout the boat.

His quick eye and long experience guided him as he made his observations. "Range, seven thousand yards. Angle on the bow five degrees starboard. Estimated speed, twelve knots. Down scope." He couldn't risk the periscope being up more than a few seconds because it cut lightly into the wave pattern. If the oiler had good lookouts, they could spot the white "feather" of a periscope.

Like a sixth sense, Raff felt the *Mako* and her crew become alert, ready to do battle. He wanted to get to about a thousand yards from the oiler before firing. He raised the scope again briefly, then again, to determine its course, range, and speed. Charlie read the angles from the top of the scope. Paul dialed them into the TDC for transmission to the torpedo gyros.

"Make ready tubes three and four. Final bearing and shoot! Up scope!" Raff lined up the periscope on the target, checked the tanker's bearing one last time as he gave the command to "Stand by three," then "Fire three!" Five seconds later, by a stopwatch, he ordered, "Fire four!"

Dead silence. Raff knew there would be no warning, no sign to the men on the tanker that this beautiful morning was about to end for them forever. *Quick death is best,* he thought. Then *KaBLAAAM!* Five seconds later came the shattering sound of another hit: *KaBLAAAAAMMM!*

Raff raised the scope. The first fish had exploded under the oiler's bridge, blowing the bow off, while the second took the complete stern. Its midsection wobbled, then the oil on board ignited with a low *BLOOOM* sound. Flames roared up into the air. Nothing that resembled a ship remained.

It was time for the *Mako* to take evasive action. "All ahead full, depth . . . ," began Raff, but suddenly, he was flipped into the air and thrown onto the conning tower floor. The loudest explosion Raff had ever heard went off right beneath the *Mako*'s bow.

A Betty had seen the glint of the submerged submarine in the tropical waters and dropped a depth charge with—nearly— deadly aim.

Raff scrambled back to his feet and shouted out his orders. "All compartments check for damages! Take us way down. Depth, three hundred feet. Rig for silent running."

Reports began to come in over the intercom. "Forward room to control, no damage in the forward room." "After engine room to control, no damage in the after engine." "Pump room to control, no damage to pumps." One by one, Raff visualized the parts of the *Mako* as the reports came in, nodding in relief that the boat was intact. *This was some rugged shark of a submarine,* he thought. Still he wondered, *How could that explosion be so loud and close and do no damage?*

Tom Benson sat near Raff. Through his headphones he could hear the whines and clicks of sea life gliding above them: porpoises and a far-off pod of whales. These were friendly, reassuring sounds of nature. But from a distance, perhaps from a base onshore, came a rhythmic whisper.

"Cap'n, I hear screws. A destroyer, I'd guess."

"One of those Bettys must have radioed for backup," replied Raff, his voice low. "All ahead full. Let's put some more distance between us and that destroyer."

Tom pulled his earphones off so that his eardrums wouldn't be damaged. They could all hear it now. No need for sonar. A rising sound like the panting of some robotic animal. *Thwap. Thwap. Thwap. Thwappa-thwappa-thwappa. THWAPPA-THWAPPA-THWAPPA!*

The destroyer had to be directly overhead to be that loud. Raff waited for the sounds that would tell him the destroyer, three hundred feet above them, was making figure eights. That was the usual search pattern before dropping depth charges. Not the dainty swirls that Liz made at the ice arena. Raff felt a pang of homesickness for his wife. Would he get home?

The destroyer paused. It didn't begin a loop for a figure eight. Raff instinctively looked upward.

Click . . . BLAAAM! Click . . . BLAAAM! Click . . . BLAAAM!

A string of depth charges rocked the *Mako*, making her bounce like a bath toy in the dark ocean depths. They were close and loud; they had to be very near misses for the *Mako*. Was it dumb luck that the Japanese had dropped them so close to a target they couldn't even see or hear? And what about that first depth charge, the one the Betty had dropped—there was something about that, something Raff's mind was trying to frame, but he had to attend to the crisis of this moment.

Cork insulation flew in little globs off the bulkhead. Tools clattered to the floor in the control room from a ruptured locker. Some tubing from the intercom system broke free of its mounts and bounded out like a snake into the conning tower. Raff used the backup communication routing to bang on a call button for damage reports. But again, the damage was minor all through the boat.

Charlie's eyes met Raff's. They gazed steadily at one another as Charlie asked in a low tone: "Cap'n, do you suppose the Japs have some new contraption for searching? Some super sonar? They weren't even pinging, and look how close they got."

Raff shook his head. Not in denial, but puzzlement. Was that the explanation? This was going to be the toughest evasion he'd ever done. He'd need to play it smart. And he'd need all the luck in the world.

Maybe the *Mako* could duck under a blanket. "Control room, can you find me a thermal?"

"Negative, Captain," came Paul's reply. "We're watching real close, though."

Raff clenched his jaws. Time for some fancy maneuvering. "Helm, give me a knuckle to starboard."

Eddie Haverly had helm duty. He veered sharply to the right. But they were not confused. Another string of depth charges rained down on the *Mako*.

Click . . . BLAAAM! Click . . . BLAAAM! Click . . . BLAAAM! Click . . . BLAAAM!

Raff steered left and right, port and starboard, but still the depth charges followed. Raff knew it was only a matter of time before one would hit. He had done all he could to avoid it, but it was going to happen. And it would kill them.

Then, suddenly, all the depth charging stopped. Was it a miracle? Raff saw Benson's face light up in hope. But Raff knew something else had to be happening. No one spoke. No motors, no pumps, no vents—no sounds at all. Steam dripped from the ceiling of the stiflingly hot compartments.

CLANK . . . CLANK . . . CLUNK CLUNK . . . CLANK! Raff shivered and startled at the sudden, unfamiliar noise overhead. Those weren't depth charges.

"For'd torpedo room to control. We are experiencing a loud

A KNUCKLE

A "knuckle" is a sharp, sudden turn, which churns and swirls the water, creating a false shape for Japanese sonar to ping and hiding the true location of the submarine.

clanking noise moving aft down the starb'd side of the hull!" Each compartment reported the same message until it reached the after torpedo room. Then it was gone. A small *thunk* came from the rear of the submarine.

Eric Edison called up from the open hatch into the conning tower. "Losing my bubble! Stern is rising! I can't adjust!"

Like a lightning bolt to his brain, Raff knew everything. Knew the *Mako did* sustain damage with that first explosion from the Betty. The seal on an impulse bottle above one of the torpedo tubes must have ruptured. Each of those bottles has four hundred pounds of air stored in it to propel a torpedo toward its target. The *Mako* was laying a trail of bubbles on the surface!

The Japanese destroyer knew precisely where the boat was from the bubble trail. Their first strategy had been sinking, then they must have realized how valuable a captured submarine would be. They could learn hundreds of secrets to give them an edge in the war.

Sinking and dying in the ocean's depths was a price every submariner had always known he might need to pay. But a war submarine must never be captured. All else could be sacrificed to prevent that. And Raff Abbott would.

But not without a fight.

The pursuing ship on the Java Sea's surface had dropped an immense grapnel hook 300 feet down and attached it to the *Mako*'s starboard stern guard. They were going fishing, planning to reel in the *Mako*. They could not know the skipper of this sub was a superb fisherman himself. And this submarine was the *Mako,* named for a shark many fishermen try to catch, but few succeed in doing so.

"LOSING THE BUBBLE"

A curved glass gauge, filled with liquid, indicates the sub's angle of incline in the water. "Zero bubble" means the keel is parallel to the ocean floor. An "up" bubble is a rise of the bow over the stern. A "down" bubble indicates the stern is pointing upward. "Losing the bubble" means the planesman can't hold position at the ordered angle (such as "half down bubble") and instead the boat is at, for example, "one down bubble."

Raff poured power to the screws. "Rudder amidships! Full dive on the planes! All ahead full!" As the power surged into the screws, the *Mako* began to vibrate and shimmy, but the grapnel held fast. The submarine began to rise.

"All stop" was Raff's next command. He knew his batteries, source of their power and life support, could not last long with such demand. He would use the weight of added seawater to the stern to halt the ascent.

But even tons of seawater did not slow their rise. They were only 250 feet down now.

Raff called for a knuckle to starboard, and then to port, thrashing on the end of the hook like a fish wildly trying to escape. He ordered all available crewmen to the rear of the boat to weigh it down. Still the *Mako* rose.

Edison called out, "We're at one hundred feet from the surface!" the marker Raff had dreaded. But he was prepared.

He would commit suicide.

Raff would order the death of his sub, his crew, and himself. "Prepare to destroy the boat," he ordered.

Everyone knew what they must do. Knew there was little time left to do it in. Sparks and the other radiomen took sledgehammers and began smashing the decoding equipment. Smitty, Kaluza, and Paul tore maps and reports to shreds. Gunners went into the torpedo rooms to position fifty-five-pound charges of TNT between the warheads of the reload torpedoes. When these were detonated, both torpedo rooms would be blown to bits. Ocean water would roar into the submarine.

They would join the *Oarfish*, after all.

Around Raff the crew prayed quietly, or nodded at one

another in a solemn good-bye as they continued with the destruction. Charlie reached for Raff's hand to shake it, as he had back on their first day together in Wisconsin, watching the submarine being built. Eons ago, or was it moments ago? Raff felt the same sense of trust and confidence again. It fueled him, steadied him. Inspired him. He did what should not—logically—have made sense.

"Flood *forward!* Left full rudder! All ahead emergency!" The *Mako* thrashed like an angry shark biting on its hook, a living thing with a fierce and uncanny ability to survive.

Without warning the hook broke away and the *Mako* swam free.

Raff sank to his knees. Then he laughed.

Out of sheer joy to be alive.

L O C A T I O N: Under the Java Sea
Enrique Romero
Things Not Done

"Nicky! Nicky, wake up! The hook's off. We're not going to
scuttle the boat. We're going to make it!"

Enrique propped himself up on his elbow and leaned across
the aisle between bunks. He whispered earnestly into Nick's
ear: that big, flappy ear he'd yanked on so many times.

"I don't think he can hear you," murmured Owen, who had
crawled into an empty bunk behind Enrique.

Nick had been unconscious through the struggle with the
hook. That was a good thing. A few times Enrique had seen
him convulse in pain, and mumble. "What are you trying to
say, Nicky?" he'd asked. Helping Nick helped Enrique keep
from being scared. But Doc said sometimes wounded guys just
babble and it doesn't mean anything.

The only words Enrique could make out were "farm" and
something about "Mom" and "pretty." He was sure that wasn't
babble.

"How is he now?"

Eric squatted down next to Enrique and Owen.

"About the same. I don't know if he's dreaming, or what,

but he's trying to say something. What's going on in control? It feels like we're diving deep again."

"Yup. Haverly just relieved me. Cap'n says we must've popped an impulse bottle from a torpedo tube and left a bubble path. That's how the Japs knew just where we were. But he said the bottle must be about out of air now."

Enrique nearly whistled in amazement, even though it's not Navy to whistle. "Wow! There's no way we'd have found something like that looking for damage in the torp room. So does he think we've lost them?"

"Nope. They're probably hopping mad about us wiggling off the hook. They'll stay up there pinging us all day unless they get orders to go someplace else."

"We'll have to stay down till nightfall?" asked Owen, with dismay.

"Yeah, it's not even noon," added Enrique. "Nicky needs some fresh air to heal up. It's so hot we can't keep the sweat off him. Owen's been dabbing a towel on him, but it's not helping much. Can't they turn on the ventilation?"

Eric shook his head. "Too noisy. We're on silent running. Besides, we've got to conserve our can. Or else . . . Well, you know."

Enrique's eyes widened. He'd been so busy worrying about the hook, and Nick, and his own leg hurting, that he didn't remember what he knew all too well.

The battery charge was wearing down. Twisting and turning to get off the hook had used up huge bursts of amperage. Without battery power, they had no life support. Without battery power, they couldn't surface. They weren't in the clear yet.

Click . . . BAAM! Click . . . BAAM! Click . . . BAAAAMM!

Eric lost his balance and fell hard against Owen's bunk.

"If we could just fire back, it wouldn't be so bad," Eric growled. "Run screaming at them and waving our guns, like the Army guys do. Feels like we're just ducks in a shooting gallery and they're loading up to pick us off."

Owen and Enrique nodded. Through the mist that had formed in the humid compartment, Enrique saw Doc materialize, weaving his way between bunks. He'd been bringing salt pills to everybody to make up for the sweat they were losing in the heat. He was also gathering and sharing news, trying to keep up morale. Enrique saw a weary smile on Doc's face.

"Good news. Mr. Zelks says there's a lot of current in these waters, mostly down deep where we are, and running southeast. That'll bring us closer to Fremantle. And away from that destroyer up there. We'll coast on it as much as we can."

"Hey! Yippee!" Enrique felt a surge of hope.

"Owen, Nick needs some sugar water. Go make up a mixture. Half a teaspoon to a cup of water. I've got an eyedropper to feed him with. And get the rest of us anything you can find to eat."

Owen slid out of the bunk. "Sure thing." He looked relieved to have something to do. Owen was out of the compartment when it started again:

Click . . . BAAM! Click . . . BAAAMMM! Click . . . BAAAAMMM!

Nick startled from the noise and the sharp dip the *Mako* took from the shock of nearby bombs. He moaned loudly, struggling against the cords that held him in place in the bunk. Blood erupted from his side, soaking the bandage around his waist and bubbling up like a geyser. Doc lunged toward Nick, frantically probing with bloody hands for where to apply pressure and stop the hemorrhaging. Nick coughed. Blood and some thick stuff oozed out of his mouth. He sputtered. Then his eyes flew open. He looked wildly up at Doc, then at Enrique, who dragged himself, with Eric's help, over to Nick.

"Hang in there, Nicky!" said Enrique, sliding his hand under Nick's shoulder. He was scared, but he didn't want Nick to be.

"Am I . . . going to . . . ?" began Nick in a voice that sounded like something inside him was gurgling and leaking.

Enrique felt his throat constrict. "We're getting close to Australia, buddy," was all he could say.

Nick's body relaxed. He looked not with pain but with surprise at Enrique. "I won't get . . . a . . . chance to . . . the farm . . . what I learned . . . bring . . . Mom . . . didn't think . . . this would . . . happen." The last word came out almost as a yelp, like a newly birthed animal. Enrique saw a soft, puzzled look in his friend's eyes, which turned slowly into a glassy stare.

Nick Gallagher had died in his arms.

L O C A T I O N: Under the Java Sea
Owen Pasquerly
Gifts

Owen's lungs expanded to gather in as much of the hot, thin air as could fit inside him. He didn't care that it reeked of diesel oil and battery gas and the morning's hash browns. He was intent on getting through the after battery room and the mess into the galley. He ducked around the hot machinery and past exhausted sailors in shorts with towels wrapped around their heads.

Smitty was already in there, opening cans of diced fruit, lunchmeat, cranberry sauce, juice, crackers, and anything else he could find to pass around. He glanced up at Owen and nodded.

"Men gotta eat. Even with the bombing going on. Helps take their mind offa it. How's Gallagher doing back there?"

"Not so great. Doc sent me here to make up some sugar water for him. And to get some chow for the guys."

$P-I-N-G$ $P-III-NNNN-GGG$

Smitty frowned at the bulkhead. "Wish that fast current they're talkin' 'bout would drift us away from here. That pinging's got a good fix on us again. We'll probably get another close string of depth charges. Hang on tight to those fixin's so you don't drop 'em. Here. I'll take some and follow you on back if we can swing through the control room first."

The floor was slippery with gray slime: a mix of sweat dripping from bodies and condensation from valves and pipes. Owen and Smitty passed out food to Billy, Sparks, and Al as they squatted in a corner. They were waiting to take their turn at the planes and the helm.

After fifteen minutes a fellow's arms and legs would tremble so much from the heat and bad air that he couldn't continue. Through the humid mist that clouded the control room, Owen saw Eddie's skinny arms struggling to hang on to his big red wheel. Next to him, Tom had wound a rag around the stern planes wheel to keep a better grip. Tom jerked his head in Owen's direction and gasped, "How's Gallagher?"

It scared Owen to say again what he'd said to Smitty. The danger Nick was in reminded him of all the things that could happen.

Click . . . BAAAM! Click . . . BAAAAAMMM! Click . . . BAAAAAMMM!

Smitty skidded on the wet floor and landed on his rump. A few crackers snapped when he hugged them to his chest, but nothing dropped. Owen gave Smitty a hand to help hoist him up.

They passed food up the conning tower ladder and to the engine crew, then ducked down through the small door to the crew's quarters. A lot of guys were in their bunks with their eyes closed. Not sleeping, but trying to shut out the terror of the depth charging. But Owen didn't even look at them. His heart bounded out of his chest at the sight of Enrique. Tears streamed down Enrique's face. He wasn't even trying to hide them.

Owen lunged over to Nick's bunk, spraying crackers, sugar water, and fruit in all directions. "Gallagher? Gallagher!" he gasped, already knowing Nick could not answer him. Could not be alive, or Enrique wouldn't be crying, not caring who saw.

From the other end of the compartment, Buzz sprang up from his bunk. He swayed like a drunken man and began to laugh a cackling laugh as he glowered at Owen and Enrique.

"You dumbbutts. Look at you. A baby and a damn pedro. So your pal died. So what? Stop that blubbering. Stop it! Stop it! We're all of us gonna die down here. We're dead men! Ahhhh!"

As Gretz began to scream, Smitty joined his thick, powerful hands into a great fist and slugged Gretz on the back of his head. Gretz crumpled, unconscious, like a marionette whose strings had been cut.

"I didn't know you hated Gretz, too," said Enrique in a low, flat voice.

"Don't hate 'im. I've served with worse. Just that yelling's dangerous. Japs can hear, and it's catchier than measles. Can't have a whole boat of us carrying on."

Owen began to laugh as he pictured Smitty and the captain and Sparks and all the other guys squawking and screaming. He pushed his hand into his mouth to keep from making noise. He was surprised when he pulled it out to see that he was crying. Just like Enrique.

Enrique was bending over Nick. He slowly reached to touch Nick's ear. "It doesn't seem like it's actually . . . him," said Enrique in a wondering voice.

"Well, it ain't him. Not altogether," replied Smitty. Doc nodded as he said: "Something's gone. Besides just his heart stopped beating, and all."

"Way I think of it, my *Oarfish* buddies will keep him company," said Smitty, patting Nick's bloody, stilled body.

"But we'll take care of him proper. With respect, won't we?" asked Owen in a small voice.

"Let's plan it," said Smitty, firmly. "How about we take the top off a mess bench to lay him on? It's thin enough to pass up the hatch."

"And then what?" asked Enrique.

"It'll be a burial at sea," said Eric. "We'll have a ceremony topside for him."

BLAAM! BLAAM! BLAAM!

The *Mako* bounced and swayed again, but this time not so hard. "I didn't hear any clicks!" said Owen.

"That's good. Means they're not so close. We're probably drifting on that current. Maybe there's a blanket in here, too," said Doc, gazing around at the bulkhead, a look of relief on his sweaty face.

"So, what about Nick. What else?" asked Owen.

"We'll unzip his mattress case and put him inside. To keep him covered up," said Smitty.

"I wonder if . . . we could . . ." began Owen.

"Could what?"

"Could we put some things inside there with him?"

"We'll put some gun shells in. To weigh it down. So he can sink down into the sea," said Doc.

Smitty looked at Owen. "That ain't what you meant, is it?"

Owen looked at Enrique. They spoke at the same time.

"The shells are good—so he doesn't just float. He should sink down. Yeah, that's good. But besides that, we want to give him some of our things. That we like—that he'd like."

Blaam! Blaam! Blaaaam!

They hardly noticed the depth charges.

"Should we make a list?" asked Smitty.

"My silver mustache comb. That's real nice. Nicky used to kid me about my girlfriends. I got that from a girl," said Enrique.

"How about we put some of his diagrams of the sub in? He was really good at that. Wouldn't have been long before he qualified for dolphins," said Eric.

"I got dolphins. I'll give him mine," said Smitty.

"I don't think you can give your dolphins to anybody," said Doc.

"Don't care about regulations. Dolphins is what I've got for him," said Smitty hotly. "He deserves best we can give him."

"What Nick liked best of mine was doughnuts. Guess that would get all soggy, though," said Owen.

"Soggy's OK," replied Smitty. "He'll know you meant it for something good."

L O C A T I O N: The Java Sea
Owen Pasquerly
Enrique Romero
Southern Cross

"Stand right here, Pasquerly. Right under the main induction," said Ace to Owen. "What do you smell?"

Owen crowded in among a bunch of guys, their heads thrown back, laughing crazily and sniffing the air whooshing down the main induction shaft.

"It's lilacs! Lilacs! Just like the bushes at home," said Owen, amazed.

Ace howled, flexing his arm like he always did when he was happy, making his hula-girl tattoo bump and sway. "That's the sweetest smell in the world!"

At last, the *Mako* was able to surface. The conning tower hatch and the main induction over the engines had been thrown open. Clean night air flooded into the submarine. After the stale, foul air they'd breathed for twelve hours, their confused senses told them lilacs were raining upon them, lush and beautiful.

"Coming through. On your left," came the bossy voice of

Eddie Haverly. Owen looked around to see Eddie leading the prisoner. His hands were chained behind him. There were reddish marks where a gag had been tied over his mouth. Owen knew that was to keep him from shouting during the depth charging, to help the Japanese zero in on the *Mako*. Now, Eddie had the duty to exercise the prisoner.

Had Enrique seen them yet? How would he react? Owen turned to follow them.

Enrique sat in a bunk, hunched over, as Doc and Smitty lifted Nick's body into the mattress cover.

The prisoner stood still, ready to resume the stares of hatred he and Enrique had exchanged in the forward torpedo room. But Enrique looked impassively at the Japanese sailor. Owen watched as the prisoner gazed at Nick's body, then back at Enrique. His look was different now. There was no sympathy. But no fire, either.

"Let's move on," said Eddie, poking the prisoner in the ribs.

"You still . . . hate him?" asked Owen.

Enrique shook his head. "I guess I . . . don't have much of that left. Being so angry. Juan died, and now Nicky. I should be two times as mad. But . . . I . . . don't know. This war. There's too much dying in it."

"Eddie told me that prisoner kicked on the bulkhead when we were being pinged." Owen thought it was important to tell Enrique this, in case he'd forgiven the prisoner too soon.

Enrique sighed. "I'd have done the same thing."

"It's time to put anything inside with Nick now," said Smitty.

Enrique looked down at what had been collected. A cowboy

story from Eddie. Some playing cards from Tom. Nick's diagrams that Eric had gathered up. A sugar doughnut from Owen. Smitty's dolphins. His own silver mustache comb.

"Owen, would you go get all the guys? They should be here for this."

Enrique, Owen, Tom, Eddie, Eric, and Smitty stood topside, on the deck alongside Nick's body. Mr. Anderson slowly unfolded an American flag and spread it over Nick. Captain Abbott said some words. They were good words, thought Enrique, about giving their shipmate to the sea for eternal rest. But he'd rather have heard the Latin and Spanish words they would have said back home.

The gunners pointed upward and shot a four-gun salute. The sound seemed to go up and out forever, under the stars. Then Sparks, who had stayed below, played a record of "Taps," the mournful trumpet farewell that honors a dead sailor.

After that, there was just wind and darkness and silence. Then, the six friends tipped the bench on which Nick lay. He slid into the Java Sea, alone, except for the small gifts from his friends. Enrique watched as Nick melted into the black water.

"We're still in enemy territory," said the captain. "Anyone not on watch duty, get below."

Enrique felt himself get hot and panicky. He couldn't go down yet. He had something to say to Owen, something to be said under the night sky.

"Permission . . . please, sir . . . could Pasquerly and I stay a little while longer?"

"All right. But lean on him or the bridge. That leg of yours still needs healing. And don't be long."

"What is it?" asked Owen, after the captain and the others had moved away from them.

"I figured out what Nicky was trying to say. Back when he was just getting out a few words. Then again before he died."

"What was he saying? About getting back to help on the farm?"

"That was a little of it. But I remember he told me, after being on lookout on a night like this one, that he'd got an idea of what would make his mom happy. He was planning on getting her a pearl necklace. He . . . wanted me to help pick it out. That's how I know."

"That was nice of him to think of his mom."

Enrique began to talk fast, in case they ran out of time.

"Don't you see? That's the one thing I can do for him now. We'll get paid when we go on break in Fremantle. I'm going to get that necklace. I'm going to hang this whole starry night—Nicky's last night in this world—around her neck. After the war is over, before I go back to my folks, I'm going up to Minnesota and I'm going to take it to her. And I'm going to put it on her."

Owen didn't reply. His face became thoughtful. Then he said, "I'm coming with you. She was nice to me. Back in New Orleans, before we left stateside. And remember, Nick was my friend, too."

Enrique said, "Are you sure you want to?" He thought how, suddenly, Owen looked older. Like he'd grown into himself.

Owen nodded. "That's what I'm going to do. Who knows? I

might even stay in Minnesota. Open my own bakery. I'll send some money to Ma to get a train ticket to visit me there. Pop, too, if he'll take it."

"You'd do that for your pop? I got the feeling he wasn't very good to you."

"Yeah, but, I remember when he was nice. Maybe he remembers how to."

Enrique and Owen turned as they saw Mr. Zelks approach them. "Don't mean to intrude," he began, "but, there's something I wanted to show you, since I saw you looking up at the sky. Do you see, there? That set of stars?"

He traced his finger in the air in a long line, then a short line across it. "That constellation's always been seen as a good sign by sailors. It's the Southern Cross. It'll guide us to Australia."

"Are we still going to Australia, sir? Now that Nicky . . . now that we don't need to get him to a hospital?"

"We've got a smashed decoding machine. Can't receive or send any messages. Our maps are in shreds. We've got a damaged torpedo tube. We took quite a pounding back there. We need to go in for repairs."

"We still have to go through the Lombok Strait," murmured Owen. "Nick's sharp eyes steered us through there. He won't be here to help us this time."

"No, he won't. But this time we'll be heading away from danger, not toward it—I think it's time for you to go below now, sailors."

Enrique and Owen nodded. As Enrique leaned on him, hopping and dragging his leg toward the hatch, Owen looked again at the sky. At the Southern Cross. Leading them to safety. Leading them home.

Aerial view of a fleet submarine

Author's Note

Owen, Enrique, Nick, Raff, Smitty, and the others on the U.S.S. *Mako* are fictional characters. My hope is that they come alive in these pages, as a way to honor the real submariners of World War II, one of whom is my father.

Most of what is in this story either did happen or could have happened. Characters, incidents, dialogue, and technical details grew from what sixteen WWII sub vets told me; from my weekend on the U.S.S. *Cobia* (now part of the Wisconsin Maritime Museum in Manitowoc); and what I learned from published accounts.

Like Owen, some sailors were underage. Falsifying birth records was a way to get away from home and serve overseas.

Most Mexican American servicemen were placed in the Army; large numbers were sent to the Philippines and other Pacific campaigns. But, like Enrique, some served in the Navy, on submarines and other ships.

Sailors from big cities had bunk mates from farm communities; Northerners worked with Southerners, perhaps for the first time in their lives. It was an environment ripe for personal growth and expanding one's horizons, as well as a setting for danger.

The chapter "Guns and Bread" is based on a real encounter of the U.S.S. *Blackfish*, with Paul Cummings as boarding officer. Like Owen, the *Blackfish* baker was both a crack shot and provider of the bread that made the peaceful resolution possible.

The second battle in this story, in the "Convoy" chapter, is modeled on a spectacular battle fought in July 1944 by the U.S.S. *Parche* ("Ramage's Rampage" in *Challenges of the Deep: The Story of Submarines*).

Captain Raff Abbott painfully visualizes the ways in which his *Oarfish* companions could have died. The agony of slowly realizing that the U.S.S. *Tirante's* sister submarine has been sunk is movingly recounted in *Submarine!* by Edward L. Beach.

The final battle of this story includes captain's directives, damage and preparation for self-destruction from the harrowing struggle of the U.S.S. *Thresher*, when it was hooked and very nearly captured by the Japanese.

I wish the reader smooth sailing. May you have a steady ship and never lose your bubble!

Partial list of sources

Beach, Edward L., *Submarine!* (New York: Henry Holt and Company, 1952).

The Bluejackets' Manual (Annapolis, MD: United States Naval Institute, 1943). (The sailor's essential handbook.)

Calenberg, Jerry. *U.S.S. Cobia at War* (Unpublished manuscript compiled for the Wisconsin Maritime Museum, 2001).

Calvert, James F. *Silent Running: My Years on a World War II Attack Submarine* (New York: John Wiley & Sons, 1995).

The Cook Book of the United States Navy Bureau of Supplies and Accounts (Washington, DC: United States Government Printing Office, rev. 1945).

Fluckey, Eugene B. *Thunder Below! The USS Barb Revolutionizes Submarine Warfare in World War II* (Urbana: University of Illinois Press, 1992). (The reader gets a wonderful sense of this skipper's personality and there are poignant descriptions of rescued Australian and English POWs.)

Galantin, I. J. *Take Her Deep! A Submarine against Japan in World War II* (Chapel Hill, NC: Algonquin Books, 1987). (There are some particularly vivid descriptions and bits of dialogue in this memoir by the skipper of the *Halibut*.)

Hoyt, Edwin P. *Bowfin* (New York: Avon Books, 1983).

Kimmett, Larry, and Margaret Regis. *U.S. Submarines in World War II: An Illustrated History* (Seattle: Navigator Publishing, 1996). (This book is invaluable for its many photographs and diagrams.)

Lent, Henry B. *Submariner: The Story of Basic Training at the Navy's Famed Submarine School* (New York: Macmillan, 1962). (Although written after WWII, much of what is described in this book would have been the experience in the 1940s.)

McLeod, Grover S. *Sub Duty* (Birmingham, AL: Manchester Press, 1986). (The great majority of submarine memoirs are written by officers. This account is by a torpedoman, and is uniquely valuable for obtaining an enlisted man's point of view. Though it contains some "adult" language and situations, it is probably the most accessible memoir of this type for young people.)

Mansfield, John G., Jr. *Cruisers for Breakfast: War Patrols of the U.S.S. Darter and U.S.S. Dace* (Tacoma, WA: Media Center Publishing, 1997). (A compilation from many eyewitness accounts, this is an adventure story of sister wolfpack submarines.)

Michno, Gregory F. *U.S.S. Pampanito: Killer-Angel* (Norman: University of Oklahoma Press, 2000). (This book concentrates, through interviews, on the reactions of the crew to their marginally competent captain, and on their rescue of seventy-three English and Australian POWs.)

Morin, Raul. *Among the Valiant: Mexican-Americans in WWII and Korea* (Los Angeles: Borden Publishing, 1963).

Nature's Masterpieces (London: Reader's Digest Association, 1994). (See pp. 64–65 for photographs of marine phosphorescence.)

Sasgen, Peter T. *Red Scorpion: The War Patrols of the U.S.S. Rasher* (Annapolis, MD: Naval Institute Press, 1995). (A very useful history of a Manitowoc-built submarine.)

Weiss, Harvey. *Submarines and Other Underwater Craft* (New York: Thomas Y. Crowell, 1990). (This is one of a number of nonfiction books on submarines for young people, although fiction titles for this age group are nonexistent.)

Wheeler, Keith, and the editors of Time-Life Books. *War under the Pacific* (Chicago: Time-Life Books, 1980). (This volume contains terrific photographs of both U.S. and Japanese submarines.)

FILMS

Destination Tokyo. Despite some inaccuracies, this is a wonderful war-era movie. It inspired men to become submariners, including Fred Richards, the underaged sub vet who assisted with *And the Baker's Boy Went to Sea.*

The History Channel's film series on Mexican Americans and war.

The Silent Service. A four-part series on the History Channel profiles the boats, the captains, the attack plans, and the torpedoes of WWII submarines. Includes archival footage and interviews with many sub vets.

Submarine Warfare. This compilation of three documentary films, with footage of submarine warfare during, and shortly after, World War II, portrays the grimy, sweaty, cramped environment as no Hollywood remake can.

WEB SITES

www.ussubvetsofworldwarii.org
www.subsowespac.org
www.maritime.org
www.wisconsinmaritime.org
www.ussnautilus.org

To order a copy of this book, please send payment and the following information to:

Sparkling Press, 137 E. Curtice St., St. Paul MN 55107

sparklingpress@peoplepc.com

Send to:

Name: _____

Address: _____

City: _____ State: _____ Zip: _____

Telephone: _____ e-mail: _____

Is this the address where you receive your credit card bill? ____

If not, please list that zip code: _____

$16.95 (for Minnesota address, $18.14)

Add $4.00 for shipping and handling

____ Check if you wish copy autographed, and any inscription:

GROUP SALES: With the purchase of 15 or more copies, receive free an equal number of copies of "What Was it Like?" a collection of quotes by WWII submariners

PAYMENT: __ Check __ Money order
          (make out to Sparkling Press)
__ Credit card (VISA or MasterCard)

Card number: _____

Expiration date: _____

Last 3 numbers on the back of the card:_____

Name on card: _____

Cardholder signature: _____